Streets and Alleys

Streets and Alleys

Stories with a Chicago Accent

Syd Lieberman

August House Publishers, Inc.
LITTLE ROCK

Published 1995 by August House, Inc.,
P.O. Box 3223, Little Rock, Arkansas, 72203,
501-372-5450.

Printed in the United States of America

10 9 8 7 6 5 4 3 2 1 HB

LIBRARY OF CONGRESS CATALOGUING-IN-PUBLICATION DATA

Lieberman, Syd, 1944-
Streets and alleys: stories with a Chicago accent/ by Syd Lieberman.
p. cm.
ISBN 0-87483-424-4 (hardbound: alk. paper)
1. Chicago (Ill.)—Social life and customs—Fiction. 2. Jewish families—Illinois—Chicago—Fiction. 3. Autobiographical fiction, American. 4. Family—Illionois—Chicago—Fiction. 5. Jews—Illinois—Chicago—Fiction. 6. Domestic fiction, American.
I. Title.
PS3562.I4413S77 1995 95-23740
813'.54—dc20 CIP

Executive editor: Liz Parkhurst
Project editor: Rufus Griscom
Design director: Ted Parkhurst
Cover design: Harvill Ross Studios

The paper used in this publication meets the minimum requirements of the American National Standard for Information Sciences—Permanence of Paper for Printed Library Materials, ANSI Z39.48-1984.

AUGUST HOUSE, INC. PUBLISHERS LITTLE ROCK

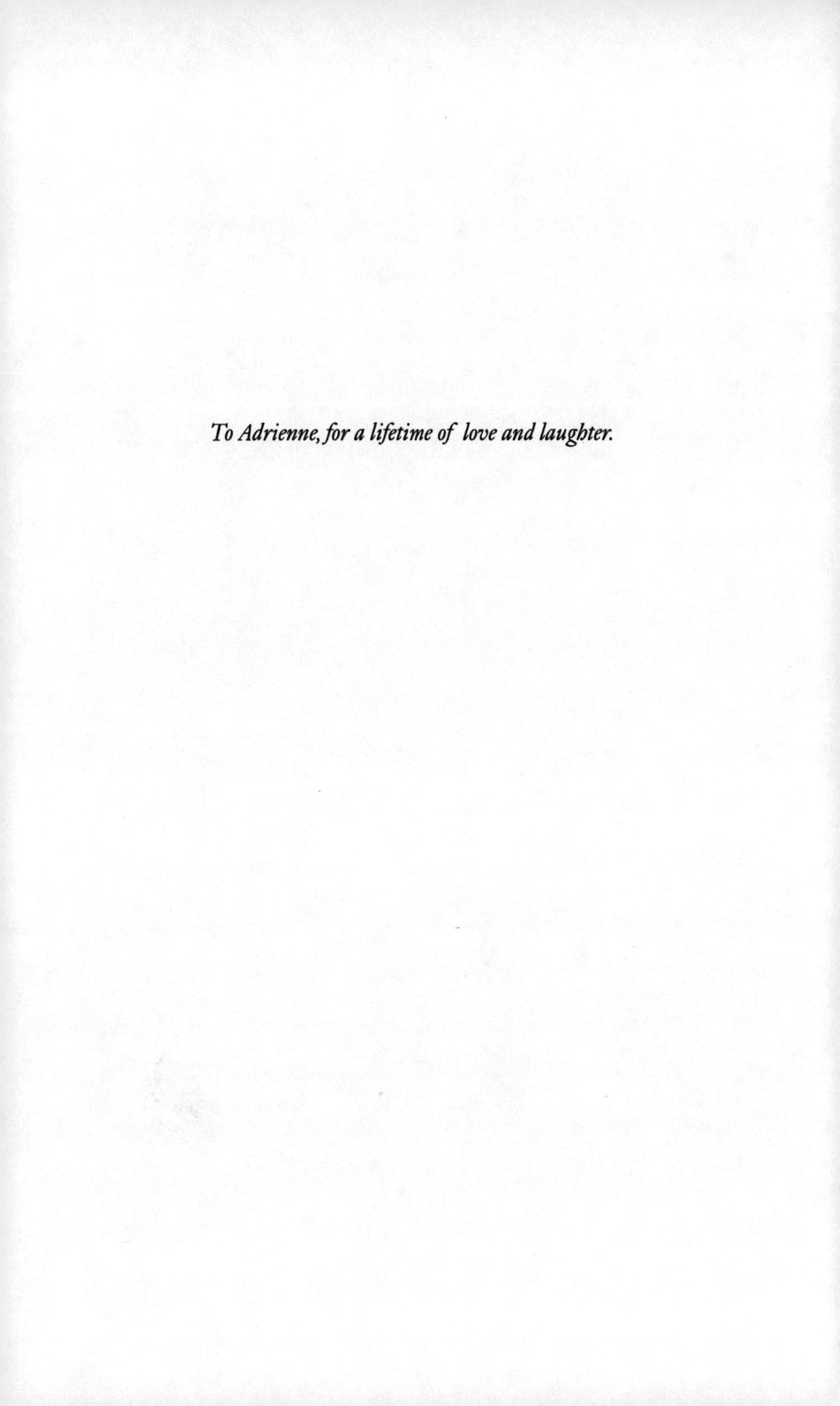

To Adrienne, for a lifetime of love and laughter.

Contents

―

Acknowledgments

I was amazed when I watched my wife write her first book. It seemed an impossible task. Now that I have finished my own, I realize that an author brings a book to fruition only with a great deal of help.

Jimmy Neil Smith and the National Storytelling Association have created a flourishing storytelling community that nurtures me. Many friends in this community have encouraged me throughout my career: in particular Clare Cuddy, Heather Forest, Joan and George Goldman, Beth Horner, Nan Kammann, Jim May, Peninnah Schram, and Ron Turner.

Special thanks to Lynn Rubright, who inspired me to become a storyteller in 1982, and who has served as my guru and mentor ever since; to Joyce and Byrne Piven, who for five years taught me the ins and outs of performing; to Jay O'Callahan, who showed me the power in personal stories and who encouraged me to write my own; and to Ed Stivender, who taught me a lot about laughter and who also introduced me to Ted Parkhurst, president of August House, with the Stivenderesque line: "Have you met pressless Syd Lieberman?"

I'm pressless no more. With the help of my agent, Jane Jordan Browne, I alighted at August House, a true home. Liz Parkhurst, vice-president and editor-in-chief, not only encouraged me, but also suggested how I might transform oral tales into written ones.

Rufus Griscom, managing editor, tightened up my prose and helped me weave my stories together to create a whole.

I'm grateful to Evanston Township High School for being flexible about my teaching schedule. And I owe special thanks to Gene Stern, my department chairman, for encouraging me to use storytelling in my teaching.

Watching my children, Sarah and Zach, grow up showed me the importance of capturing the magical moments of life through story. Along with their inspiration, they've given me loads of joy.

My biggest thanks go to my wife, Adrienne. She encouraged me to take on the project and held my hand whenever it seemed beyond me. More important, she served as a sounding board for my ideas and an editor for all my work. Without her fine ear for prose, her absolute honesty, and her tireless efforts, I could never have produced this book.

Introduction

People sometimes express pity when they hear I grew up in the city. But on the streets and alleys of Chicago, I stalked flying grasshoppers and made them spit out their tobacco juice before I let them go. I fed ants to spiders and then fed the fattened spiders back to the ants. I explored the ravine-like passageways between buildings. I pretended that the ice cream sticks I floated down the street's gutter in rain storms were rafts on the Amazon.

There must have been girls living on our block, but I don't remember any. Our streets and alleys were a boy's world, where we trained to be hunters and warriors. All year long, we ran and threw and hit and hid.

In the fall we played football in the street. The curbs defined what was out of bounds, and the parked cars played an important role in the game. "Bernie, go out to the blue Pontiac and stop. Al, cut between the Chevy and the white Dodge." Since I was one of the youngest kids on the block, they always sent me long.

In winter we hid behind those same parked cars, waiting for an unsuspecting driver to happen by so we could jump out, grab the bumper, and get towed down the snowy street.

In spring we broke out our bikes and held races around the block. Pity the pedestrians who strolled onto our raceway.

In summer we played Lineball in the streets and held a summer-long pinners tournament in the alley behind my apartment building. The tournament ended with a world series the week before school started. I became the youngest winner ever the summer I turned eleven.

My mom would shoo me out of the house each morning. Except for meals, I wouldn't return until after dark. At night we played Ring-o-Leveo, a hide-and-seek marathon that ended only when our mothers called our names in the night. Then we would rise up from our hiding places, and end the game with our own call: "Olle, olle, ocean free. Olle, olle, ocean free."

When I returned home at the end of each day, my ankles wore a ring of dirt. After washing, I'd fall into bed with my ear pressed against the radio, trying to catch a Cubs' road game. Sometimes I'd tune in to "Jammin' with Sam," a black rock and roll show my brother discovered one night at the far end of the radio dial.

But streets and alleys were more than just the playing fields of my childhood. As I grew, they provided the landscape where I grasped the lessons that turned me into a man, lessons about winning and losing, right and wrong, lust and love. Like my childhood apartment, my house now sits on a street and an alley. There I've watched my kids grow up and learn their own lessons.

In my elementary school gym, we used to play a game called Streets and Alleys. In that game, rows of kids line up with their arms outstretched and their fingers touching. The passages between the rows are streets. One person chases another down the streets, trying to tag him. When the leader calls "alleys," the lines turn ninety degrees, opening up new passages perpendicular to the first. Every time streets turn into alleys or alleys turn into streets, the whole landscape changes.

As I wrote this book, I'd look down one street and suddenly find myself in an adjacent alley, remembering a story that I had forgotten. I was surprised both at the stories that demanded to be told and at the ones that will have to wait for another book. Toward the end of her life, my grandmother presided in the lobby of a hotel, waiting for a family wedding to start. Her children and grandchildren swirled past her with greetings and kisses. Gram motioned toward the tableau and, in a voice filled with wonder, said, "That's the way my life goes." Having written these stories, I now know how she felt.

A Winner

On the morning of my father's day off, he'd preside at the kitchen table, poring over the racing form like a scholar scrutinizing the Holy Bible. A study in absolute concentration, he never glanced up, even as he wet his finger to turn the page.

Pa would spend the afternoon at the track, and the evening at the trotters. If he were lucky, he'd join the all-night card game in a back room of a neighborhood cigar store, playing until dawn or until he was broke.

But Pa never sat in on many all-night card games. That's because he had no *mazel,* no luck, when it came to gambling. If Pa bet on a baseball game, his two outfielders would pull an Alphonse and Gaston routine—the ball would drop between them, and the winning run would score. His quarterback would fumble away the winning touchdown as he went over the goal line on a quarterback sneak. The basketball stars he bet on would miss game-winning slam dunks.

Two Yiddish words describe an unlucky person: *shlemiel* and *shlimazl.* The *shlemiel* is the person who spills soup on the way from the kitchen to the table, and the *shlimazl* is the person the soup lands on. When it came to gambling, my father was both.

One of Pa's favorite bets was the quinella. It offered a big payoff because you needed to win five races in a row. One day Pa had won four races and had two horses alive in the fifth. His horses were the two favorites in the race. If either one came in first, he stood to win $15,000. Finally his ship was going to come in.

In the home stretch my father's two horses were running first and third. Usually he would watch the races quietly. But that day he was snapping his fingers and beating his program on his leg and yelling at the horses and urging the jockeys on.

Of course, the horse that was running second beat them both by a nose in a photo finish. Pa stared at the tote board in amazed silence. "Just my *mazel*," he finally said quietly. "Let's go home." On the way home, he started to go through a traffic light and thought better of it. He backed up right into a police car. They gave him three tickets: damaging city property, reckless driving, and running a light ... backward.

Pa's dead now, but I know he's still gambling. How else can you explain the 1985 Bear's NFL playoff game in which the Giant punter went to kick the ball and missed it, giving the Bears their first touchdown? The television announcer started laughing. "In all my days of playing and broadcasting, I've never seen anything like this," he said. "How could that have happened? My God, how could that have happened?" Well, I knew how it had happened. My father in heaven had taken the Giants.

I remember so many losing days and nights. He'd leave in the morning after going to the barber, all slick and full of hope, and return in the evening, a tired, beaten man in need of a shave. But on the days he won, the look on his face and the feeling in the house were magical. It was as if the gods were looking down on us and everything was right in the world.

When I was nine, I decided to test my own luck. Some of the older kids on the block were going to Riverview, Chicago's old amusement park, and my mother had agreed to let me go with them. She gave me money to spend on rides and then handed me some extra. "For lunch and snacks," she said. "Have a good time." I pocketed the extra money, knowing exactly what I wanted to do with it. Buying food wasn't part of my design. I was my father's son; I was going to play the games of chance to see if I was lucky, to see if I could win.

My father was going to the track that day, so he sat at his customary spot at the kitchen table, reading the form.

"Aren't you going to say good-bye to your son?" my mother asked.

He looked up for a brief second. "Be careful," he said and then quickly returned to his studies.

"Good luck, Pa," I replied.

He waved without looking up.

Riverview was a Chicago landmark. The old amusement park opened in 1904 as a shooting preserve for men, with a merry-go-round for the women and children. By the time I started going there in the early '50s, Riverview had grown into the world's largest amusement park, the two-and-one-half mile circular midway packed full of rides and games. It wasn't like the theme parks we have today, where all the workers look like dropouts from prep school. Riverview was a place with a seedy, carnival atmosphere, a place deliciously exciting for a little kid. It was filled with games of chance.

I went with Alan Dresden, who always seemed to have a runny nose; Jackie Mages, who had grown a few inches over the year and was all gangly arms and legs; and Sidney Goldblatt, the only guy in our crowd who was shorter than I.

As soon as we got there, we burst through the gates and ran down the midway. It didn't matter where. At every turn we could find a ride that would scare us or drop us or spin us or bump us. The scarier, the higher, the faster, and the harder, the better.

Aladdin's Castle, the fun house, was always our first stop. From beneath his jeweled turban, Aladdin himself stared at us from a painted backdrop, daring us to enter. In we went, through a maze of screen doors. About thirty seconds into the maze, I knew I could never go back the way I came in. Dresden got completely lost. "How did you guys get so far?" he shouted, pushing against one screen door after another that wouldn't move. "Wait for me."

But I didn't. I always wanted to be alone in the castle so no one could warn me about what was to come. I quickly plunged on through corridors so dark I had to feel my way along the walls. The corridors twisted and turned. People's screams punctuated the silence as mechanical monsters lit up or sprang out of the wall. A moment of relief came when you entered a lighted room with a slanted floor and funny mirrors.

You only exited the castle once, to walk up some stairs. The staircase was a gantlet for women because a man in a hidden booth would press a button and a blast of air would blow the girls' skirts up à la Marilyn Monroe. I usually loitered at the bottom of the stairs, pretending to be waiting for my friends, but actually hoping to catch a glimpse of panties.

On this day, though, I was too excited. I took the stairs two at a time and back in I went, through a huge rolling barrel, across patches of floor that spun in all directions, and down another series of dark tunnels. The fun house ended at Aladdin's magic carpet. I sat on a bench that broke and rode a conveyor belt out into the sunlight.

As I waited for the others to show up, I played my first game. I tried knocking over a pyramid of milk bottles in three tosses and almost won. I had to knock down just two bottles with my last toss, but the pressure got to me and my throw went wildly off to the left. The fat carny that ran the game pushed three balls toward me as he tried to talk me into trying again. But my friends beckoned me on.

The next hour was a blur of old wooden roller coasters—the Greyhound, the Blue Streak, the Silver Flash; crashing bumper cars; and the Pair-O-Chutes, a ride where you were dropped as you sat under an actual parachute.

By midmorning, we were ravenous. Mages and Dresden ordered hot dogs. Goldblatt was already picking at his cotton candy with his fingers. I satisfied myself with a small Coke.

"Not hungry?" asked Mages as he smeared mustard down the side of his bun.

"Naw, not yet," I lied.

Goldblatt smiled a sticky smile at me. "Need any money?"

"I'm not hungry," I repeated. I thumbed the lunch money in my pocket, trying to blot out the smell of the food with images of all the games of chance that were sprinkled throughout the park.

Dresden popped the last piece of hot dog into his mouth and wiped his nose on the back of his hand. "Want to try the Bobs, now?" It was Riverview's biggest and fastest roller coaster.

"Naw," replied Mages, "Shoot-the-Chutes comes first."

"Race ya," yelled Goldblatt, tossing the rest of his cotton candy into the garbage can as he took off. Dresden came in last, laboring to breathe all the way. Mages, still trying to figure out how to use his new arms and legs, came in a distant third. Like two water bugs, Goldblatt and I scurried between people, fighting for first. He won by a nose. I hoped it wasn't an omen.

We took our seats in a long boat at Shoot-the-Chutes. When everyone was in, a man at the back poled us down a dark tunnel. Then an elevator lifted the entire boat to the top of a water slide. At the top you could see all of Riverview. My friends were pointing out all the rides: "There's the Rotor" ... "Look at Whip-the-Whip." Meanwhile, my mind was on all the games: "I'll shoot free throws for sure." ... "Maybe I should try the mechanical monkey race" ... "Damn, there's where I missed the milk bottles."

Then down we went, gathering speed, the spray wooshing over the sides. When we hit the pond, we screamed as a big wave drenched us. I tapped Goldblatt who was sitting in front of me and pointed a few rows up. A teenage couple was soaked. You could see the outline of the girl's bra against her dress.

"You know where they'll head next," I said.

"Yep," Goldblatt answered, "Want to follow?"

Who could resist?

It wasn't by chance that the Tunnel of Love lay just opposite Shoot-the-Chutes. The wet twosomes would go in, hugging to keep warm. Goldblatt and I followed the couple. Like movie private eyes, we kept ducking behind people so that we couldn't be seen. We got on a boat just a few rows behind the couple. We weren't on the water long before they began to hug and kiss.

"Darling," I cried to Goldblatt, "I love you. Kiss me. Kiss me." I made smooching noises and threw my arms around him.

"Sweetheart, I love you, too," Goldblatt yelled.

Several people laughed, but even in the dark, I could see the guy's neck turn red.

We exited quickly, darting in and out of the crowd and hiding behind a couple of trees. The guy came out first, fists clenched. He glanced up and down the midway. To keep from laughing, we held our hands over our mouths. Finally, his girl managed to drag him away, but not before he gave one last mean look in all directions, just in case we were nearby.

We caught up to Mages and Dresden playing Skee Ball. It was my friends' favorite game. "Watch this," yelled Dresden as he wound up and rolled a small ball down an alley. At the end the alley curved up and the ball leaped into the air and landed in the one of several concentric circles, for a varying number of points. "Yes, a fifty," he shouted and threw again.

"I got one hundred points last turn," said Mages, who was rolling nearby.

Goldblatt was waiting his turn. When he saw that I wasn't going to play, he looked incredulous. "You sure you don't need some money?" he asked. "I've got plenty."

"Nope," I replied. "I'm fine. I'm going to the john. I'll be right back."

I hated Skee Ball. The way you won was by collecting points. So many points gave you so many tickets. But if you saved your tickets all summer, if you saved your tickets for a lifetime of summers, you never earned enough tickets to actually win anything. It was like being an indentured servant. I wanted to win now.

But so far I was having my father's lousy luck. I almost won something shooting free throws, but my last shot bounced off the rim. I just missed dropping a hoop over a Kewpie doll's head. "Tough luck," said the carny, as he jingled the change in the pouch he wore around his waist. "Want to try again? Come on, I'll give you some tips." But they didn't work. My next tosses weren't even close. "Sorry," he said and moved on to a new customer.

Things went from bad to worse. I couldn't hit anything in the shooting gallery. The mechanical cars I bet on finished last. My darts weren't even close to popping a balloon. I grew desperate, beginning to play games I knew I couldn't win. I even tried Ring-a-Bell, a game where you hit a pad with a mallet, hoping to drive a metal ball high enough to strike a bell. Most men couldn't do it. I knew what my father felt like, playing long shots in the late races just to break even.

I hit bottom when I lost at the Fish Pond, a baby game where you fished with a plastic fishing pole, trying to catch a plastic fish with a star on the bottom. Everyone won at that game, but there I stood feeling completely foolish as four- and five-year-olds pulled up the plastic winners. Every bottom I turned over was as empty as my stomach.

I had only a quarter and no confidence at all left when I

approached the final game. Located close to the exit, the Nickel Toss was a small booth whose painted border had pictures of spinning nickels on a red and blue backdrop. A wire mesh screen stood about a foot off the floor, and on the screen were green glass ashtrays. You threw your nickel through the air and if it landed in a green glass ashtray you won it.

I played this game every time I came to Riverview with my parents, and my house was filled with green glass ashtrays: in the kitchen, in the bathroom, in the living room. And my parents didn't even smoke in the house. It was as if a green glass monster had wandered through our apartment leaving his droppings. But that didn't stop me, because I wasn't after the green glass ashtrays. I was after something bigger. There in the center of the booth, rising like the monolith in the film *2001: A Space Odyssey*, stood a pillar. On the top of the pillar was a plate glass. If you landed your nickel on the plate glass, you could pick anything in the house. I had seen nickels hit the plate glass and bounce off, nickels hit the plate glass and slide off, nickels hit the plate glass and disappear. It was a black hole for nickels.

But so what? Every time I threw a nickel through the air, I was doing just what my mother said my father was doing. I was throwing my money away. Yet the brief time of flight was a time of hope, a time when the gods might crown me a winner.

I got five nickels from the bored carny and took my position. My first four tosses were swishes, not even a green glass ashtray. Dresden complained that he wanted to go. "Just one more toss," I said without looking back.

I took aim, whispered a silent prayer, and tossed my last nickel into the air. Rising in slow motion, it looked like a flying saucer, perfectly flat. Up and up it went, without a wobble, my hopes rising with it. Everything else disappeared: my friends, the crowd, the carny, even the booth itself. My world became that nickel in the air.

At the apex of its flight, I knew it had a chance. I held my breath.

It sank so quickly that when it hit the glass, I was startled. It bounced high into the air and I thought it was going to fall to the floor. No, no, I thought, Please, no. And then, somehow, it landed again dead center and stayed there.

My mouth fell open; I couldn't talk. Everything stopped; everyone seemed frozen. Then my friends began to shout and jump all over me. The carny came to life. "We got a winner here," he shouted and waved his arm to the people strolling by. "Hey, come on over! We got a winner here! A winner! A winner here! This kid just won anything in the house!"

His patter worked. A huge crowd gathered around me. One man even shook my hand. When the carny felt he had a big enough crowd, he announced, "This kid just won anything in the house." He leaned toward me, "So, kid, what do you want?"

What did I want? How should I know? I had never gotten that far. All I had wanted to do was win.

People began to shout advice. "Take the stuffed bear." "Look at that darling giraffe." "I'd take the huge gorilla." A man in a bowling shirt leaned toward me, took a dead cigar out of his mouth and whispered, "Don't take a stuffed animal, kid. There are pans up there. They're worth a lot of money. Take a frying pan. Take a roaster."

But I didn't really need any advice. As soon as I scanned the shelves, I knew what I wanted. On the top shelf, way off on the right, stood the object of my desire, my reward for winning, the laurel crown that the gods were going to place on my head in triumph. It was a lamp!

But not just any lamp. This lamp's base was twisted in tortuous shapes. It was a driftwood lamp. Actually, it was a fake driftwood lamp made out of plaster of paris. It was a heavy, fake driftwood lamp made out of plaster of paris and it was painted shiny chocolate brown. It seemed exotically beautiful to me.

When I pointed toward the lamp, the man next to me raised his eyebrows and shrugged. But I didn't care. "Good choice," said the carny. I hugged my shiny, chocolate brown, heavy, fake, plaster of paris, driftwood lamp to my chest and passed through the cheering crowd. My friends were gaga. The lamp was half my size. It was the greatest thing any of us had ever won.

We took the bus home. I had to explain to several smiling passengers how I had won my driftwood lamp.

When I got home, I ran into the house and shoved the lamp into my mother's face as the whole story tumbled out. Then, in an act of kindness I don't expect to be equaled in this lifetime, she removed one of the green glass ashtrays from a table in the living room, and set the lamp down.

I couldn't wait for my father to get home. When he came in, I played it cool. I sat in the living room by the lamp and waited.

I heard him in the bedroom removing his pants. That meant he had lost and wasn't going out that evening. He entered the living room in his underwear and slumped into his chair. I still didn't say a word. "What's that?" he asked.

"I won it," I said proudly.

He smiled for the first time since he came into the living room. "At least one of us won," he said. I beamed brighter than my lamp.

We spent a typical evening at home. My teenage brothers took off with their friends. My father fell asleep in his armchair. My mother read the newspaper while I watched television. But the light from my new lamp seemed to cast everything in a special glow. The apartment seemed cozier, my family somehow more important. "Remember to turn it off," said my mother as she went off to bed. "It's quite a lamp."

We had it for years. I'm sure it was a conversation piece. Then one day, when I was a teenager, the lamp disappeared in one of my mother's spring cleanings. But by then it didn't matter. For all those years, every time I walked into the living room, I clicked the lamp on, and every time I walked out, I clicked it off. It was proof that the gods had smiled upon me, that I had been lucky, that I was a winner.

A Real Live Naked Girl

Winter or summer, school night or holiday, we hung out at the "J," Albany Park's Jewish Community Center. The tiny building housed rooms for arts and crafts and a pint-sized gym. But what drew us was the lounge, even though it consisted of no more than a linoleum floor, some broken-down couches, and an old record player.

In the lounge we herded together, ogling the girls and being ogled by them in return. We discussed them, analyzed them, fantasized about them. We reveled in macho boy talk: "Hey, look at the pair on her. Man, I wouldn't throw her out of bed."

Before puberty, life had been simple. The year was defined by its seasons: baseball, football, and basketball. Then girls performed a silent coup in our lives. One day they were obstacles to be pushed down on the school play lot during recess. The next day, they had become the center of our world, magnets that drew or repelled us at their whim.

So at sixteen, instead of hanging out in the J's gym shooting hoops, we sat in the lounge, careful to look casual and cool. We carried breath-freshening spray, and surreptitiously tested our breaths every chance we got.

I was checking out Susie, the cutest girl in the room, as she chattered away with some of her club sisters, when Kenny stepped into my line of sight. He wore his usual smile—a smirk that said, "I know something you want to know."

"Syd," he said, "Can you get your old man's car this week?"

I motioned to Kenny to step aside. "Why?" I asked, leaning to one side when he wouldn't move.

"Can you get it?" he repeated, stepping back in front of me.

"What's the big deal?" I asked, leaning the other way.

He stepped back into my line of sight, demanding my undivided attention. "Yeah, I can get it," I said, "Wednesday night if my dad loses at the track that afternoon. Otherwise he'll go to the trotters. But I don't want to drive around all night trying to pick up girls."

Kenny looked around to make sure no adult was in the vicinity. He saw Toppel and Kuznitsky, two of our buddies, and motioned them over. They were both tall and lanky but the resemblance ended there. Toppel was dark and quiet. Kuz had red hair and freckles and often erupted into laughter over his own jokes. When the two arrived, Kenny whispered, "I heard that in La Porte, Indiana, there's a carnival with a strip show where the girls strip all the way."

Kuz giggled. "No way," he said.

"That's bullshit," chimed in Toppel as he plopped down next to me.

"Hey, that's what I heard," said Kenny defensively. "The carnival's only going to be there this week. If Syd can get the car, we can check it out." The three of them looked at me.

I knew it was a crazy idea. La Porte had to be at least seventy miles away. What if the car broke down? What if I got into an accident? What if we got arrested for being at a strip tease? What if we got lost and didn't get home until 3 A.M. My mother was always up in bed waiting for me to come in, pretending she had just woken up. At that hour my usual prisoner-of-war routine—the one where I reveal as little as possible—wouldn't work:

Mom: "Syd?"

Me: "Yeah."

Mom: "I woke up when I heard you at the door. You're just coming in?"

Me: "Yeah."

Mom: "Where did you go?"

Me: "Out."

Mom: "What did you do?"

Me: "Nothing. I'm going to bed."

But when I piled all of those problems on one side of the scale and laid on the other the thought that I might see a naked woman, it was no contest.

Here's why. Girls had always been a subject of complete mystery and fascination to me. I began wondering about them when I was very little. I wondered why they went in pairs to the bathroom in elementary school, why they stood with one arm behind their backs holding onto the other arm's elbow, and what they were talking about when they whispered in each other's ears and giggled. But mostly I wondered what they looked like without any clothes on.

Like most boys, I would sneak into the bathroom and pore over lingerie ads in newspapers and magazines. But that only made matters worse. I'd walk down streets at night, looking up at the windows, praying that fate would provide me with a glimpse of a naked woman. I'd try to look up skirts, hoping a girl had forgotten to wear her underwear. I'd make up elaborate plans to hide in a locker in the girls' locker room. I'd even scan *Mad Magazine*, in the mad hope that the illustrator had—for some unexplained reason—inked in the real thing on one of the sexy girls he drew. I find it hard to believe now, but I was so obsessed that I once checked under the skirt of a department store mannequin.

It's probably because I didn't have sisters. I grew up with two older brothers, so I understood men. We liked sports, wrestled with each other (in inappropriate places, said my mother), and didn't clean up after ourselves enough (mom again). We were loud and crude. I looked up to my brother Al for a lot of reasons, not the least being that he could belch on command.

Of course, by the time I was sixteen, I had seen pictures of naked women, but my darkest secret, the one I shared with no one, was this: not only was I still a virgin, but I still had no idea what a real live naked girl looked like.

"What do I tell my parents?" I asked Kenny.

"Tell them you're going to the J," Kenny said.

THE LIE SLID EASILY out of my mouth. Right after dinner I coolly asked, "Can I have the car?"

"Where are you going?" yelled my mother from the kitchen.

"To the J," I yelled back.

"You might want to put gas in the car," my father said as he handed me the car keys. I thought, you should only know how true that is.

The night was warm, the sky clear. We were sixteen, feeling immortal, and as we headed out of Chicago on the road that would take us to La Porte, we howled like wolves at the stars.

The ride was vintage adolescence—a radio blasting, dirty jokes, wrestling matches in the back seat, whistles and taunts hurled out of windows. The thought that naked women lay at the end of our odyssey was enough to send us through the roof.

We could see the carnival's lights from the highway. Even from that distance, it held the promise that Pleasure Island had for Pinocchio.

An old man directed us to park in a field. "Hicksville," muttered Toppel.

"Hicksville, Shmicksville," said Kenny. "A naked woman is a naked woman."

As soon as I stopped, Kenny leaped from the car and started to run toward the midway. "Watch out for cow pies," joked Kuznitsky, but the lights and crowd had already swallowed Kenny up. I got out and carefully began to make my way toward the carnival. An enormously fat woman waddled by, breathing heavily. She dragged a bawling little girl behind her.

"There are families all over here," said Toppel disgustedly. "How can they have a strip tease?"

"Damn it," growled Kuznitsky, no longer in a happy mood.

"Let's check it out," I said, hoping against hope that they were wrong. But when I saw the carnival, my spirits sank. It brought to mind the traveling carnivals you see on city side streets, raising funds for a local church.

The place reeked of wholesomeness: a small Ferris wheel, a tilt-a-whirl, a merry-go-round. In a cordoned-off area, a sad-looking pony plodded in a small circle with a beaming child on his back. Everywhere you looked, people with crew cuts and bouffant hairdos were fingering dollops of cotton candy. Even the carnies, trying to round people up to play the games of chance, seemed like clean-cut farm boys.

"We drove all this way for nothing," I grumbled as we walked down the midway.

"Kenny," Toppel said, as if the name explained everything.

Just then Kenny walked up, grinning like the Cheshire cat. "Follow me, fellows," he said. We looked at each other in amazement as Kenny began to dodge through the crowd. Soon he was running full speed and we were charging after.

At the edge of the carnival, Kenny stopped and stared off into the darkness. "There," he said, solemnly. We followed the direction of his lifted finger and saw, sitting about one hundred yards away, in the center of a cornfield, our Mecca—a small tent glowing with light and promise. "And we're in luck," said Kenny. "The show is about to start." We looked at each other, grinned, and raced across the field.

The man who took our money at the door didn't question our age. He barely looked at us. I slipped inside and saw a sea of men seated on low wooden benches. Straw was spread out on the floor. A small platform up front served as the stage. Two spotlights attached to the tent's center pole lit this area, leaving the rest of the tent dark.

We took our seats, dead center, about three quarters of the way back. "Good seats," said Kuznitsky as if we were about to see a theatrical production.

The crowd was young, but we seemed to be the youngest ones there. Though most of the guys looked to be in their twenties there were several middle-aged men in the crowd and even a couple of old geezers. "Jesus," whispered Kenny, "look at that old fart. He's liable to have a heart attack when they start stripping."

Expectations ran high; the place hummed with nervous talk. Seated next to me was a bearded man, who appeared to be in his forties or fifties. He wore blue jeans and a work shirt. His gut spilled out over his belt as he leaned forward, resting one forearm on his thigh. When he saw me looking at him, he spit chewing tobacco juice out at his feet and looked away.

In front of me, two guys in their twenties were surreptitiously passing a bottle of whiskey between them. "Hey, kid," said the fat man next to me, tapping one of them on the shoulder. "If you don't give me a swig of that rotgut, I'm going to have to tell your mommy where you've been."

The guys laughed and one handed him the bottle. "Much obliged," he said, as he rubbed the top and took a swig. He motioned the bottle toward me, asking if I wanted some. I couldn't resist. I took only a small sip, but the bourbon set my mouth on fire. "Thank you," I managed to wheeze as I handed the bottle back to him. The old guy gave me a fatherly smile.

I felt great. Having lied to my parents, I was sitting in the middle of an Indiana cornfield with whiskey on my breath, desire in my heart, and a stirring in my loins.

"Big night tonight, huh?" he asked. I nodded, trying to control the burning in my stomach. Suddenly, he bellowed toward the roof, "Going to see me something tonight." The tent erupted with laughter and whistles. I felt as if I were blushing. He had just yelled what was on my mind. The crowd began a rhythmic clapping. "Strip tease … Strip tease … Strip tease."

I read excitement on my buddies' faces. Kenny glanced at me. "Pretty soon," he said, rubbing his hands.

Then without any introduction, the music began and a young girl came out, wearing a halter top with a jean jacket over it and shorts. The stripper had a good figure and long blond hair.

In seconds she had her jacket off and was twirling it over her head. "Toss it here. Toss it here." Shouts came from all directions.

She smiled, looking as if she were enjoying herself, and continued her bump and grind. "I've got other things to toss later," she yelled. Guys applauded, hooted, whistled. Then one guy, dressed like a cowboy, leaped onto the stage and started dancing. The stripper stopped. Someone cut the music.

The crowd began to boo, but she quieted us with a wave of her arm. She turned toward the cowboy. "Mister," she said, "I'll dance for you, but I won't dance with you. Now if you want to see the rest of what I've come to show you, you had better sit down." The place broke into applause.

"Sorry, Miss," the cowboy replied with that kind of exaggerated politeness found only in the South and small towns.

"That's OK," she said as he returned to his seat.

She waved and the music began again. The crowd whooped. In seconds she had tossed her coat and removed her halter top. There were her breasts, large and beautiful. A tassel hung from each breast. It was enough for me just to see them, but she was a strip tease artist.

She began to swing the tassels in circles—small circles, large circles. She spun them slowly. She spun them quickly. And then somehow she spun them in opposite directions. She had trained her breasts! I was awestruck. Some guys were giving her a standing ovation. She blew kisses in response.

The whole time she stripped she smiled a kind of shy, enigmatic smile as if she were proud of her hold over us and also astonished by it. She had me mesmerized.

When she tossed the tassels, I just missed grabbing one. I felt as disappointed as I had when I was younger and had missed catching a foul ball at a Cubs game. One of the guys in front of me caught it. He held it up to the stripper and kissed it. She winked.

When she started to unzip her shorts, I held my breath. But she seemed to think better of it and zipped them back up. Several guys groaned. I was among them. She turned then and as she revolved her hips slowly, she started to undo her pants again. Once again she pulled them back up. The crowd's groan got louder. So did mine. I had no pride left; I was ready to beg her to go on. She teased us with her shorts again and again. By the end, I was a complete wreck. I didn't know what to do; I would have promised her anything. I was ready to crawl up there on my knees and offer to help her take them off. I glanced over at Kuznitsky. He looked as crazed as I.

Finally, to thunderous applause, she let her shorts drop, danced out of them, and kicked them to the back of the stage. She turned and except for her G-string she was completely naked. My mouth hung open. I couldn't believe that only a thin strand of material stood between me and what I longed to see.

Seconds ago I had reveled in the sight of her breasts, but now that wasn't enough. I wanted more than anything to have her drop that G-string. In my concentration I don't remember the crowd cheering or applauding. I don't even remember the crowd. I couldn't see anything but a few inches of her body.

I felt as if we were alone, as if I were King David and she were dancing for me—a woman all curves and mounds and a secret place. And then suddenly, she dropped her G-string and her secret place wasn't secret anymore.

Some firsts you never forget. This was one of them. I studied that v-shape of hair with the reverence one reserves for greatness, and when I looked up, she was smiling, I swear, right at me.

When I came back to reality, I found myself on my feet with all the other men. Guys were applauding, whistling, slapping hands, hugging each other. I began to hoot and rap Kuznitsky on the top of his head. He never looked away from the stripper.

"I told you so, didn't I?" said the big guy. "Thank you, little lady," he yelled. "Thank you." Eventually she bowed and backed off the stage, blowing kisses as she went.

"Yes, thank you, little lady," I muttered to myself. "Thank you."

Other strippers followed, but they didn't count. I had already seen what I had come to see.

On the way home, the guys rehashed the highlights of the evening. Kenny provided long, lavish descriptions of what we had seen. Crude jokes bounced around the car. I ignored them and pretended to concentrate on my driving.

"We know what Lieberman is thinking of," crowed Kenny. He winked and leered at me.

I flashed him a contented, dreamy smile.

"Oh, yeah," he shouted, pinching my cheeks like a kind uncle. "Look at that smile. We know what you're thinking of."

How could you, I thought. The smile didn't leave my face all the way home.

Lights and Darks

Every June, as school wound down, I would suddenly realize that I needed a summer job. Of course, by then it was always too late to find one. So I was reduced to daydreaming that a rich uncle had found me a construction job that would mean muscles and money. I envisioned myself casually rolling up the edges of my short-sleeved shirt and telling people, "Yes, I work construction." But as hard as I shook, no rich uncles ever fell out of my family tree.

When I was sixteen, my luck changed. A new laundry opened a few blocks from my house, and a help-wanted sign appeared in the window. Working in a laundry didn't carry the panache of being a construction worker, but it meant money. Also who knows—I might deliver some silky undergarments to a beautiful woman, be invited in, and then ....

The laundry turned out to be a small storefront with two rows of washers set down the center and dryers lining the walls. "Clean-Rite Laundry" it said on the door. "N. Goldberg, Proprietor."

When I entered, the owner rose from a machine with two arms full of laundry. He was old, in his sixties, with wispy gray hair ringing his bald head. His clothes were cheap: black shiny pants and a thin shirt that looked as if he had washed it too often in one of his machines. "Yes, what do you want?" It wasn't really a question. It was a statement that said, "Get out of here. I don't trust teenagers." But I needed money, so I stood my ground.

"I'm looking for a job," I replied, hesitantly. "I live about four blocks down ...."

"Can you work nights?" He threw the clothes into a dryer, wiped his hands on a towel, and approached me, moving quickly as if he were trying physically to stop me from coming farther into his store. His eyes seem to dart in all directions. "I'm looking for a boy who can work nights. No monkey business. Hard work."

Nights! My heart sank. Nights were for the guys, cruising the neighborhood, playing cards, or hanging out in Jensen Park. I could see my summer disappearing in a whirlpool of shirts and pants.

"I'll pay $1.50 an hour. No more. I need somebody to help with deliveries. I can't get up the stairs." He walked to the window and nodded toward a three-story apartment building across the street. "Some of these people, they live on the third floor. They don't want to carry the clothes up and down. Why do you think they pay me to do their laundry? They pay me to do the schlepping. But I can't do it. I need someone maybe three hours a night on Monday, Wednesday, Friday. For deliveries. Can you work those nights?"

"Sure," I replied even though I knew Friday night was impossible. Everyone went to the movies on Friday night. Hundreds of teens invaded the Terminal theater like locusts. It was so noisy, the management would have to refund the money to any unsuspecting adult who wandered in. I couldn't spend my Friday nights delivering laundry. But I figured I would start the job anyway. I was sure I could get him to change the night after he saw that I was a good worker.

"Be here tonight and I'll give you a try," he said, dumping a load of clothes into a dryer. "But remember, you don't have the job yet. Not yet. You have to work hard. You understand? Work hard."

That night he briefed me on the job. "First you divide the clothes into lights and darks. You never mix loads. I'll take care of washing them. You take care of drying. You understand?" He was walking in front of me between two rows of washers, and he didn't wait for me to answer. "Each load is a different person. See." He tapped a piece of masking tape on top of a washing machine that read, "Mrs. Schwartz" and then moved quickly on. "Sometimes two, maybe three washers contain clothes from the same person. It's OK to put them in one dryer. But you have to look for the name." He tapped another washer. "You always look for the name before you take the clothes out and put them in the dryer. You understand?"

What I understood was how much I disliked him. After he explained the job, he never said anything to me except to tell me which washer to empty. We worked in silence. As I removed clothes from washers and put them in dryers, I watched him. Shifty-eyed and fidgety, he never stayed still, never relaxed. He reminded me of a rodent, nervous and afraid as he scurried from machine to machine.

He never looked directly at me, even when he was giving me instructions, but every time I looked up from my work, he seemed to be glancing at me out of the corner of his eye. When I caught him at it, he would quickly look away.

There was a touch of the greenhorn about him.That's what my grandmother called immigrants. She had come over to this country from Hungary, and grew haughtier the longer she was here. She felt that there was something grabby about immigrants, something mistrustful. They acted as if they had arrived in the land of the thieves instead of the land of the free. "But Gram," I used to say, "not all immigrants are like that. Look at Mrs. Kelman." Mrs. Kelman lived above us in our apartment building. She had lost her entire family in the Nazi concentration camps, but after the war she came to America, where she married and started a new family. Mrs. Kelman worked with her husband in their fish store. A loud, happy woman, she would bring us a fish now and then. Once when we caught a mouse in a trap in our house, it was Mrs. Kelman who came down and emptied it. "You are afraid of a little mouse?" She shook with laughter. "It's not even alive."

"Mrs. Kelman acts as if she's poor and your friend," my grandmother would explain, "but one day that greenhorn will buy this building and raise your rent."

My grandmother would have called Goldberg a greenhorn. The way he acted made me want to screw up his whole system. All I had to do was mix different people's loads together, and soon hordes of little old Jewish ladies would descend upon him, waving dresses in the air. I imagined Goldberg running from one to the other shouting, "I can't help you. You understand?"

After an hour of packing up laundry, we were ready to make deliveries. Goldberg had arranged the wash in boxes so that we could load them on the truck in the right order. He was looking around the store, trying to make sure he hadn't forgotten anything, when a black man entered.

I tensed because blacks didn't live in our neighborhood. I didn't have any contact with them except on the football field. The sight of one walking on the streets of my neighborhood made me nervous. What was he doing here? What did he want?

Goldberg seemed beside himself. "Yes, yes," he shouted as he rushed toward the man. "What is it?" Goldberg was practically screaming even though he was standing right in front of the man, blocking his way into the store.

The visitor was a little man. It was hard to guess his age. Perhaps he was in his forties; at any rate he wasn't young. He wore jeans, a T-shirt, and a light jacket. "Can I use the bathroom?" he asked. It was an odd request because there were restaurants around and there was no indication that the laundry would have a bathroom.

Even stranger than the request was Goldberg's response. He

stepped aside and pointed out the bathroom. It certainly wasn't out of kindness. He glared at the black man as he walked by. Perhaps Goldberg was afraid of him, afraid of what the black man would do if he said no. Goldberg continued to straighten up, but he couldn't take his eyes off the washroom door.

Soon we heard the toilet flush and the black man came out. "Thanks," he said. He pulled a cigarette from a pack. "You have a match?" Goldberg pointed to a book of matches on the top of a washing machine. As the black man made his way over, Goldberg slipped into the washroom.

He began to yell almost immediately. "Stop him. Don't let him go." He barged out of the washroom, eyes blazing. "He stole my safety razor and a tube of shaving cream."

I almost started laughing. A safety razor and a tube of shaving cream? If Goldberg hadn't looked so wild, I would have thought he was kidding.

"You're nuts," said the black man with a frown on his face. "I didn't steal nothing." He lit his cigarette and zipped up the zipper on his coat. He glanced from Goldberg to me and smiled, as if to say, what do you make of this guy? I shrugged in commiseration.

"Stop him," Goldberg pleaded. "Stop him while I call the police."

"Look, man," said the black guy. "I didn't steal nothing and I ain't going to stay here while you call no cops."

I wanted to ask Goldberg why anyone would want to steal a safety razor and a tube of shaving cream. And if he did, why would anyone care? I thought of bowing and waving the black man past me. Goldberg began to shout, "I'm going to have you arrested. I'm not afraid of you. I was afraid of the Nazis but not of you. You can't steal from me. I'm calling the police."

Goldberg made for the phone. The black man watched him and then turned to me. He wasn't smiling now. "Man, I'm getting out of here," he said. "I ain't waiting for no cops. Don't try to stop me."

It was the wrong thing to say. Something snapped in me. Until then, it had been Goldberg, a black man, and me in a ludicrous situation over a safety razor and a tube of shaving cream. I disliked Goldberg so much I was actually enjoying myself. I couldn't have cared less if the black man had actually stolen the stuff. In fact, I hoped he had.

But now that the man had challenged me, the entire situation had changed. As we stared at each other, I knew that I would have to fight him, not for Goldberg but for me. This was no longer about some lousy razor and a tube of shaving cream. It was now about manhood. I was bound to try to stop him. It never occurred to me that I could just let him go, that to fight over this was stupid. The situation was the stuff of movies and plays. We faced each other like Mercutio and Tybalt in *Romeo and Juliet*, like Marlon Brando and Lee J. Cobb in *On the Waterfront*. It was *High Noon*. "No, you're not," I replied.

I knew he would have to get by me to get out because machines lined each side of the aisle in which we stood. This wouldn't be like the wrestling matches that I occasionally fought with friends, but a real fight. I had seen only one real fight and it was scary. My brother had fought someone in an alley when I was about seven. After the first real punch, I ran home in tears. Now, for a second, I wondered if I had it in me to fight the man.

We stood there staring at each other, sizing each other up, when suddenly he tried to dart by me. But I was a football player. I threw a shoulder into the man and knocked him into one of the washers. I was surprised at how light he was. I was also surprised at how easy it was. After all, he was a man. He came at me then, swinging, but he missed. I grabbed him in a kind of bear hug and pressed him against a washer on the other side. He freed an arm and punched the side of my head. I was a bit dazed, but I stepped back and hit him with a right. It was the first punch I had ever thrown in anger. He fell to the floor and his nose began to bleed. When he started to get up, I hit him again. He crumpled and wound up sprawled between two washers. It was over that quickly.

I stood over him like an animal, daring him to get up. My fists were clenched and I was breathing heavily. I was angry: angry at him, angry at Goldberg, angry at myself.

That's when I heard Goldberg. "Good, you did good. I knew you were a good boy, a good Jewish boy. I called the police. They're coming. Here's a rope. Tie him up."

I turned to see Goldberg urging a rope at me. "I knew he'd be up to something. I knew he'd steal." He moved past me and stared at the man on the ground.

The black man just sat there, seemingly resigned to his fate. "I didn't steal nothing," he said quietly to the floor. "Why you want to get me arrested?"

"I knew you were going to steal from me," Goldberg replied. He looked at me. "You can't trust them."

"Let him go," I said. "It's just a razor and a stupid tube of shaving cream."

Goldberg looked at me with astonishment. "Let him go. Let him go? A thief! A … a …" He sputtered, unable to express the outrage he felt over this idea. "You'd help him steal from me, from one of your own people?"

I wanted to tell him I didn't feel like one of his people. I wanted to tell him that Jews should know what prejudice was. I wanted to scream; to hit him; to apologize to the man I had knocked down just to prove my manhood, a man I now realized was close to the age of my father. But all I could do was say, "Let him go."

Just then we heard the siren. The cop car roared up and a policeman jumped out with his gun pulled. "In here, officer," shouted Goldberg, running to the door. I looked at the black man and his eyes seemed to say, "Well that's it." I gave him a hand and helped him to his feet.

The cops came in and handcuffed him. They searched through his pockets and found the razor and the tube of shaving cream. I was shocked but Goldberg nodded his head as if to say, "I told you." The black man just shrugged. The cops seemed puzzled that all the trouble had been over a razor and a tube of shaving cream but didn't say anything. They took the black man away. Goldberg called after them to say that he would be down to press charges as soon as he finished with his deliveries. "Thank you, Officer, thank you," he yelled and waved as they pulled away.

"I quit," I said, as soon as Goldberg reentered the store.

"You can't quit," he replied. "We have deliveries to make."

"Make them yourself," I said and walked out.

"I'm not going to pay you," he shouted after me as I walked out into the cool summer night. "Do you hear? If you don't make those deliveries, I'm not going to pay you for this night. I'm not going to pay you. One day you'll learn. One day you'll learn."

Later that night I found myself with two friends in a typical summer night activity: riding around in Harvey's '57 Chevy, acting silly and trying to pick up girls. Toward midnight we were stopped at a light when a dark blue Ford slipped up next to us.

The driver was a greaser. With his wavy blond hair and long sideburns, he looked like James Dean. His eyes were half closed and a cigarette hung arrogantly from his lips. The rest of the pack was tucked into the rolled-up sleeve of his T-shirt. He never looked at us, but his challenge was evident. He simply revved his motor.

"Fucking greasers," said Kenny, turning to me in the back seat. He glanced at Harvey. "Let's bury him." Harvey revved his motor in reply. He worked his hands on the steering wheel. The greaser just smiled to himself.

We sat there waiting for the light to change. Kenny kept mumbling, "Greasers, fucking greasers." The revving engines growled like wild animals.

"I'm getting out," I said.

"What?" shouted Kenny.

"I'm getting out," I repeated.

"What the fuck is eating you?" Kenny asked.

"Nothing's eating me," I said.

"Then get the hell out in a hurry," said Harvey, staring at me in the rear view mirror. "The light's going to change."

I got out and slammed the car door. "Then fuck you guys," I said.

"Yeah, then fuck you," Kenny shouted

The light turned green and they laid rubber, leaving me standing on the curb. Through a cloud of smoke, I watched them squeal off into the darkness. I stared after them until I couldn't see their tail lights any longer. The night suddenly grew quiet. I stood there for awhile, unsure if they would come back. When they didn't, I walked home alone.

Life with Father

I was watching television at my girlfriend Adrienne's house when her mother announced that I had a call. My brother was on the line. "What's up?" I asked.

"You have to pick up Pa. He's in jail."

"What?" I stammered.

"Pa's in jail," repeated my brother. "And you have his car. He needs you to pick him up when he gets out."

"What's he doing in jail?"

"Don't get excited. It's nothing. He was playing cards in the bookie joint in the back of the Lawndale Restaurant and they got raided."

"I thought they pay the cops off," I said.

"They do pay off the Chicago cops, but the state police raided them. Pa says it's no big deal. The guy that owns the place is playing gin with the police chief right now. They just have to keep them until they're sure the state police are out of the area. Then they'll be released. Get down there. It's the Lawndale Station on Roosevelt Road."

"A problem?" Adrienne asked.

"Yeah," I said. "I have to go pick up my father." I couldn't tell her more. After all, her father was the epitome of hard work, the paradigm of honesty. When he was a child, he used to go out and play at 11 P.M. under the street lights because before playing he had chores to finish, a violin to practice, and Hebrew School to attend. As an adult, he became a government worker, overseeing the budgets of several different agencies. He had even founded a synagogue. So how could I tell Adrienne where I was going? How could I explain that strange moments like this were normal in my family? That this was just another episode of life with father, at least life with my father: Shmulky, Little Sam from Division and Damen in Chicago, car salesman, gambler, and petty crook. The story would have taken too long to unfold, and, like a lot of the truth, too much credulity to be believed.

PA BEGAN HIS TROUBLED CAREER early in life. In seventh grade shop class, he was planing down a board to make a piece for an end table. He kept bringing the board up to be approved by the instructor, who kept telling him to plane it some more. After twenty trips, the ten-inch piece had shrunk to an inch. In frustration, my father threw it through a window.

The teacher sent him to Principal Wilson, an old woman who always wore black. When he entered, Miss Wilson peered at him over her reading glasses as if trying to place him. "Don't you play basketball for us?" she asked.

"Yes, Miss," he answered. He had been on the school's championship team and pointed to the picture of his team that hung on the wall behind her. She looked at the picture, and then turned back to him as if to make sure. According to my father, she piled three chairs one on top of the other, climbed up, and took the picture down. "I don't want you hanging around me," she said. She threw the picture into the trash and my father out of school.

Once he was on his own, one of the first things he decided to do was to take a long drive. While his father was off working, he piled his mother, an old-world grandma type, and his five brothers and sisters, ages five to eleven, into a big touring car. Off they headed to Philadelphia.

I can't imagine what he must have told his mother to get her into the car. There was no reason to go to Philly; they didn't have relatives there. I picture screaming children, big suitcases, and lots of pots filled with things to eat. And what would he have told his father had he gotten there?

But Pa never made it. Actually, he only drove a few blocks, to a busy intersection where a policeman was directing traffic. "The policeman kept waving me on," my father said, "so I kept going and going. Finally, I ran into him. What do you expect?" he asked. "I was just learning how to drive."

Pa spent his formative years out on the street, trying to make a few bucks. His mother wanted him to go back to school and play the violin, but my father was much happier roaming the neighborhood and shooting dice.

He tried his hand at lots of jobs including delivering bread. But Pa wasn't the type to get up at five A.M.; hell, sometimes he was still gambling at five A.M. His favorite job when he was younger was driving a cab because you could hustle a little and cheat a little, especially when you dealt with drunks.

Once a well-dressed drunk flagged him down in front of the Drake Hotel. Pa didn't know the man was drunk until he got in and said, "Take me to six, two, and even."

My father drove along for awhile and then yelled back, "Where do you say you wanted to go?"

The guy was almost asleep, but he snapped straight up and said, "Six, two, and even." Then he sank back into the seat again.

So Pa drove a few more blocks, pulled over and shook the guy. "Hey, buddy," he said, "You're here."

The guy looked out the window, paid him, and got out. My father said, "Well, I knowed he ain't home, so I go down a little ways, make a U-turn and pull up. 'Cab, sir?' I said with a smile. The guy hopped right back in the car."

"You could tell drunks anything," he continued. Pa once told a drunk who had been asleep in his cab for five minutes that he had been with him for twenty-four hours and owed him $87.50. The guy paid and got out.

Actually, Pa wasn't the worst cheat. My father knew a cabby who would grab drunks who were walking down the street, shake them by the lapels and say, "You're here. That's ten bucks." More times than not, Pa's friend got paid.

Pa grew wistful when he told these stories of his youth, especially when he remembered a drunk who handed him five fifties instead of five ones. "I took one look at them bills," he said with a dreamy smile on his face, "put the cab in gear, and took off."

So in a way it was natural that he would wander into a life of crime. Pa blamed it on the economy. "It was during the Depression," he explained, "and there was no money. People were standing in line to eat apples." That wasn't for my father. He became a petty crook, joining a gang that rode around the country robbing pinball machines. It was as if he rode right onto the pages of a Damon Runyon story.

There was Whiz, who was a whiz with locks; Sailor, who had been a sailor; my father, Shmulky; and Shoes, who was just out of the penitentiary after doing twelve years. Shoes got his moniker because he once proposed throwing a jewelry salesman's sample case out a train window when the salesman wasn't looking. The train ran between Chicago and Dallas but that didn't bother Shoes. "I'll walk the whole train track to find it," he said.

The gang would leave Chicago, looking for pinball machines. When they found one, Whiz would pick the lock so they could get to the can that held the nickels. Meanwhile, the rest of the gang would gather around the machine and pretend they were playing. As my father explained it, "You couldn't stand there like a bunch of dummies." So the three of them would hunch around Shoes, shouting encouragement: "Nice shot ... Use your flipper more ... Great score." Once Whiz popped the lock, they'd grab the can of nickels, close up the machine, and take off.

Of course, it didn't always happen that easily. Late one night in Oklahoma City they happened upon a small diner with a pinball machine in the corner. The place was perfect. It was empty except for the owner who was working as the cook and waiter. They ordered coffee and crowded around the machine. But as hard as Whiz worked, he couldn't pop the lock.

As he cleaned the counter, the owner kept giving them the eye. Pa knew he was getting suspicious, so to keep the man busy, he ordered four pork chop sandwiches to go.

Meanwhile, Whiz popped the lock, but there were so many nickels in the tray, he couldn't even lift it. Whiz loaded up his pockets and went to the car. Sailor took his turn and loaded up his. Then Shoes. Pa filled his pockets, closed the machine, and yelled through the little window that led to the kitchen, "Hey, chief, are those pork chop sandwiches ready?"

The owner poked his head through the window. "Naw. I just put them on."

Pa didn't want to wait around, so he said, "That's OK. We like them rare."

The guy knew something was up and he started out of kitchen with a shotgun. As soon as my father heard him coming, he began to sprint to the car, holding his pants with one hand so they wouldn't fall down from the weight of the nickels. He put the car in gear and peeled away with bullets zooming around them.

Pa cut off on the first dirt road he came to, just in case the owner had called the police. At eighty miles per hour, they flew down one dirt road after another. Sailor was struggling to read a map with a flashlight. Suddenly, he began to tap the map with his finger as if he had found something. "Go left," he shouted. "Yeah, left, the first chance you get. That should get us back to the highway." But Sailor was wrong; the road dead-ended into a farm.

The farmer, who was plowing his fields by lantern light, got off his tractor when the gang roared up. His wife had her face pressed to the farmhouse window, and the farm dogs were barking like crazy.

Pa got out and gave a friendly wave to the farmer who was making his way slowly across the field. His wife opened the door a crack and asked, "Can I help you?" Pa could see the dogs behind her, snarling and snapping their teeth and struggling to get out.

"Yes, Miss," answered my father. "We're from out of town and we're having a little car trouble. Can we use the phone?"

The woman was smart enough to know that any car roaring up at eighty miles per hour couldn't be having too much trouble, and I'm sure my father's city gangster look of sport coat and dark shirt didn't help. "We don't have a phone," she said, slamming the door.

Meanwhile, the farmer had arrived in the yard and was peering into the car as if he were at the zoo, studying city flora and fauna. Sailor, Shoes, and Whiz were smiling and trying to look as natural as possible.

Pa figured the couple probably did have a phone and it occurred to him that the wife might be calling the police. He hurried back to the car, edged by the farmer with a polite "Sorry" and hopped in. As he slammed the car into gear, Pa said, "Hold on." He wheeled into a U-turn and immediately got the car stuck in the mud.

"What a commotion," Pa laughed when he told the story. "The engine was racing, the dogs—who were now out of the house—were barking and hurling themselves against the car; Sailor was yelling, 'Tie him to a tree. Tie the farmer to a tree;' Shoes was moaning, 'The coppers are going to get me ... just out of the joint and they're going to get me.' And the farmer was just standing there, staring at us as if we had come from outer space."

Finally, my father rocked the car out of the mud. When they hit the highway, they raced back to Chicago at hundred miles an hour.

Robbing pinball machines proved a lucrative business. The gang used to drive from Chicago to San Francisco, hitting towns all along the way. On one trip they had to drive the last three hundred miles without stopping because they couldn't fit another nickel into the car. "What a shame," said my father. "We had to pass up some nice towns." When they got to San Francisco and emptied out the car, they had $5,000 in nickels. They put the money into their San Francisco bank account, D&D Amusement, named for Division and Damen, the street corner they hailed from in Chicago.

That corner also spawned Redhawk, the neighborhood's master thief. Redhawk was a "booster," a name given to someone who boosts items out of stores. His talent was looking like an average joe—in his case red hair and glasses—and having guts. "All kinds of guts," Pa remembered warmly.

Redhawk operated by pretending he worked at whatever store he was robbing. He'd take off his jacket, roll his sleeves up, and put a pencil behind his ear. He fit right in. Then he'd begin stealing.

The first time Pa teamed up with him, Redhawk was going to bump off a jewelry store in Chicago. "Listen Shmulky," Redhawk whispered as they stood across the street from the store. "You're the lookout. This store has a little balcony. When we go in, you go up on the balcony and find a spot where you have a good view of the whole place. I'm going to get behind a counter and lift a tray of diamonds. If you see someone spot me, give me a *zimmie*."

"What's a *zimmie?*" Pa asked.

"A *zimmie,*" Redhawk repeated, as if saying the word again would make it clear. My father gave him a puzzled look. "You just shout *'zimmie,'* " explained Redhawk, "I'll know what you mean."

Redhawk worked this scheme all over the country. Once, pretending they were employees at Marshall Field, he and a partner carried a $1,500 rug down the escalator from the fifth floor. But no matter how hard they pushed and shoved, that rug wouldn't fit through the store's revolving doors. They had to carry it back up.

One day Pa was sitting on the corner doing nothing when Redhawk came by. "Want to take a little ride?" Redhawk asked. That meant a job, so my father got into the car with Redhawk and two other guys. They drove for a long time in silence. "Where are we going on this little ride?" Pa asked.

"Minneapolis," said Redhawk.

It seems that Redhawk had been up there the week earlier to rob a jewelry store, but he couldn't pull off the job. Now he was going back.

They drove all night, nine hours, so they could get there before the place opened. When my father woke up, Redhawk was slowly gliding to a stop about a half block from the store. "What the hell?" said Redhawk.

"What's up?" Pa asked, straining to see what Redhawk was looking at.

"It looks like a goddamn convention." Redhawk was already out the door and walking toward a clump of men standing in front of the store they had planned to rob. Pa and the two other gang members got out of the car and followed.

As Redhawk got closer, the men turned toward him and started pointing. For a second, my father thought there was going to be a shootout. He began to look for an alley to duck into. Then Redhawk began to laugh. "Before you knew it," Pa said, "Redhawk and these guys are all shaking hands and slapping each other on the back. I couldn't figure out what was going on."

"Fellows," said Redhawk, when my father and the other two

guys walked up, "Meet my gang from last week. They were with me when I tried to rob this same store last Thursday. They're here to rob the place, too. We'll have company."

"When the owner arrived," my father said, "he was so excited. Nine customers stood waiting for him to open up his store. He thought he was going to have the greatest day of his life. He couldn't show us enough merchandise. He kept running from one of us to the other. Of course, he didn't know we were all thieves."

It was hard to believe that my father had been a crook. After all, he was my father. And all of this had happened before I was born. But in pictures, Pa looked the part. Like Capone or like Edward G. Robinson—his favorite actor—he was a little plump, with a receding hairline. He dressed well: nice suits, a hat tilted at a jaunty angle, and a pinky ring.

By the time my memories of my father begin, his hairline had receded a great deal more and his belly was a lot larger. His appearance had softened. But Pa hadn't mellowed with middle age. He no longer was an out-and-out thief, but in a way he was still stealing. Pa worked as a used car salesman.

If you saw him sitting in the dealer's salesroom, you wouldn't have thought much of him—another middle-aged chubby salesman, smoking a cigar and reading the paper. But when it was time to make a sale, Pa was a dancer, an orator, an actor.

Sometimes he would use a hard sell on customers, needling, pressuring, even yelling at them. Once I saw him trap an elderly couple between cars by stretching out his arms and pretending he was resting on each auto. The poor couple squirmed as he harangued them, too embarrassed to say "excuse me." I think they finally gave up and bought the car just to be released.

He'd do whatever he could to make a deal, including out-and-out lying. Once, after finishing a sale, he whispered to me, "I promised the guy so much, I can't even remember what I said. The only thing I can remember is seat covers. We don't even have seat covers."

Pa could use a soft sell, too. He'd introduce himself as Mr. Lee, the agency's owner, and act as if he didn't need the sale. He'd pull out pictures and ask about the customer's family.

Pa also loved to pretend to be completely honest and explain to a customer how all the other car agencies would cheat them. Pa told them about the "bait and switch" tactics they would use and how the salesman would "bush" them even after the sale was made to get them to pay for a lot of unwanted extras. Of course, those were techniques he had honed to a fine art. Pa would look around as if to make sure no one was listening. "You go to another place," he would whisper, "and see if this doesn't happen. Then come back to me and I'll give you an honest deal."

Pa didn't know a thing about cars. He didn't even know how to check the oil, but he did know people, which made him a master salesman. A friend of his once told me, "Your father could have you look at the wall and after a half hour, he'd have you believing that there were diamonds growing on it. If a middle-age couple walked in, they were dead. Flat-out sold. A legend, your father was a legend."

He won sales contest after sales contest run by the car manufacturers. In fact, I typed all my college papers on an Olivetti-Underwood typewriter that he had won. On Sundays, it wasn't unusual for him to sell ten cars or more, and one Sunday he came home and collapsed in a chair, having sold twenty-one cars that day.

In the late forties, Pa made over $40,000 a year, a tremendous salary for those days, but we never got much use out of the money. My parents had three kids by then, and our family lived in a three-room, one-bedroom apartment. I slept in my parents' bedroom; and one of my brothers slept on the living room couch, while the other made do with a cot in the hallway. Money could have gotten us out of there, but my father had other uses for it.

Gambling always came first for Pa. In fact, my mother's own father, a gambler, had warned her not to marry my father. But my mother didn't listen; she thought she knew what it would be like married to a gambler.

She couldn't have imagined my father, though. After checking into the Morrison Hotel for their honeymoon, he slipped out and lost their honeymoon money in a card game. They had to check out the same day.

She tried to control him, to get him to use the money he won and not just lose it back, but she couldn't. He once won $6,000, enough money in the forties to buy a small house. My mother pleaded with him to buy one.

My father told her that he would think about it. He even went so far as to have her put the money in the bank. But every day he would take some out. By the end of the week the money was gone.

To a compulsive gambler, action is what counts. Money and the things it can buy don't mean anything.

Once he decided to treat himself to a two hundred dollar pair of shoes after he won at the track. The next day he went back and lost everything. A friend who was with him said, "He looked down at his feet and said, 'Fucking shoes, I could have placed another bet.' "

Naturally, money was always a problem. Pa tried Gambler's Anonymous, having heard they could help him. My mother was hopeful, but he returned incensed. "I'm not going back there," he announced indignantly. "All they do is talk. I thought they were going to give me some money."

THE POLICE STATION WAS LOCATED in a rough neighborhood that had been Jewish at one time but now was black and Spanish. The policemen were big, not fat like in every cop movie you've ever seen, but big—six feet tall and in good shape. They all wore leather jackets and carried guns.

The station looked like a set for a television series. Cops came and went. A drunk insisted that he wasn't drunk. An old black man held a handkerchief to a bloody forehead while the cop in front of him pecked at an old typewriter. There was even the obligatory prostitute. She wore a skintight miniskirt, a little lambswool waist-length jacket, and a blond Afro wig that sprang out in all directions. If I squinted, she looked like a French poodle that had just received half a shave.

I bounced into the station—a clean-cut white teenager sporting a crew cut, Bermuda shorts, and a T-shirt. When the black desk sergeant saw me, he slowly rose and leaned way over the counter. He didn't say anything but simply stared, looking as if he were seeing an apparition.

"I've come to get my father," I smiled. "He was in the Lawndale Restaurant when it was raided."

He sat back down, relieved that I wasn't a hallucination. "We released all of them a while back," he muttered. Then he plunged back into a pile of papers.

I found a pay phone and called my brother. "They were released. Where is he?"

"They're back at the restaurant," he said. "Get him there."

I drove over but the restaurant was dark. I found a pay phone in a gas station and called my brother again. "It's closed," I said.

"Pa just called. He said to tell you to go up to the window and tap on it with a coin. Tell the guy who comes out that you're Shmulky's son."

"What?"

"Just do it."

So back I went. I parked about a half a block away and sidled up to the window, turned so that I was facing the street—I had seen many gangster films—pulled a coin from my pocket, and surreptitiously tapped the window right between the "w" and "n" in Lawndale.

A short bald-headed, bearded guy ran out from the back, shielding a candle. He opened the door a crack. "What do you want?" he whispered.

"I'm Shmulky's son," I said out of the side of my mouth. He poked his head out the door and looked up and down the street.

"OK, quick," he said, "come in."

Once I was in, he locked the door and blew out the candle. We traveled in single file through the darkness and silence of that restaurant. I felt like Orpheus heading through the underworld.

The little man stopped when we reached a door and solemnly put a finger to his lips. Then he pushed the door open to reveal a sea of middle-aged men silently sitting around a jumble of candlelit tables. For a second in the dark, the scene looked like some strange Satanic ritual. Then I heard the unmistakable sound of cards shuffling. The gamblers had come back to finish the games that had been interrupted by the raid. But since the bookie joint was supposed to be closed down, they were playing silently by candlelight.

When Pa saw me, he waved me to his side. "Shh," he said, putting a finger to his lips, "we got to be quiet. We're finishing up. Sit down. I'll just be a couple of minutes." A couple of minutes! I knew that meant the rest of the night. I kissed good-bye to any thought of getting back to my girlfriend.

"I'll be right back," I said, "I have to make a call."

At dawn my father woke me up and we started home. In the car I said to him, "Pa, you're almost fifty. Don't you think you should slow down a little?"

"If I slow down," Pa said as he pulled away, "I'll die."

He never did slow down. Five years later, he volunteered to get a drive-away car from the dealership he worked for and take Adrienne and me back to college on his day off. I wondered why until he woke me at 3 A.M. somewhere outside of Cleveland to ask me where Pawtucket, Rhode Island, was located.

"What do you want with Pawtucket, Rhode Island?" I asked. "Harvard is in Cambridge, Massachusetts."

"Narragansett Race Track is in Pawtucket," he replied. "I've never been there. I've been to almost every major track in the country, but never there. Anyway, I got a friend who hangs out there that I'd like to see. They call him the Big Turk."

"Is he Turkish?" Adrienne asked.

"Naw," Pa replied, "he's Jewish. But he's big and he looks like a Turk."

Pa drove all night, one thousand miles. He made it to Narragansett ten minutes before the first race, hopped out of the car, and told me that he would meet me in Cambridge. That night at eleven Pa showed up at my dorm room. "OK, drive me to the airport," he said. "I'm catching a red-eye flight home." That's how he spent a day off at age fifty-three.

But as fast as my father ran, age caught up with him. Pa died at fifty-eight, the death of a gambler.

On his day off, he bet ten races at Arlington Park during the day and ten more at Sportsman's Park that night. Then he drove directly to the emergency room of the hospital and checked in with a heart attack. The next day Pa's luck ran out.

I was in the room when the final moments began. Pa sat up with a puzzled look on his face, as if he had received a tip on a sure thing that had run out of the money. "I can't breathe," he said. When the real fear and horror set in moments later, the doctors rushed me out.

His friends called him a legend. In a way he was. Of course, we're not talking about Johnny Appleseed crossing the country to plant trees but a Johnny Appleseed visiting every race track in the country; not Pecos Bill flying around in a cyclone but Pecos Bill cruising in a luxury Pontiac; not Paul Bunyan with an axe but a Paul Bunyan with a daily racing form. He was Shmulky, Little Sam from Division and Damen in Chicago, a car salesman, a gambler, a petty crook, and my father.

The Way to the Big Road

"Come on out and pick up the old man's car," my uncle yelled as if he had to talk louder on a long distance call. "He's not going to drive anymore. He had three accidents already this month. No more driving. He'll take taxi cabs if he wants to go somewhere. I'll take him around. The car's yours."

He slammed the receiver down, leaving me rather befuddled and a little giddy. My own car, I thought. Seventeen and my own car. It didn't matter that it was an uncool family car, a light-blue Ford Fairlane. It was a car and it was going to be mine. I envisioned myself parked at the lakefront on warm summer evenings, necking with my girl.

That night at dinner, I was still lost in that fantasy when my mother said, "Listen, he's getting old. It's probably a good idea that he doesn't drive anymore." She said more as she passed the potatoes, but I didn't really hear her. The thought that Gramp could get old seemed inconceivable to me. Sure, we called him the old man—everyone did, all of his seven children and all the thirteen grandchildren—but we said it lovingly, indicating his status in the family rather than his age. He was the family patriarch, filled with wisdom and strength. How could the old man have gotten old?

The next day I found myself on a train heading out to Benton Harbor, Michigan, where August Pohl Auto Wreckers, the family business, was located. My grandfather could thank the Czar for the route that led him to this junkyard on the edge of Lake Michigan. He'd been drafted into the Czar's army, and for a Jew, that meant a lifetime commitment. So Morris and Ethel Lieberman left Kovno Guberniya, Lithuania, in 1912, heading for America.

I looked out the window of the train. We were somewhere near the Indiana Dunes, for I could see mountains of sand in the distance. The wisps of dry grass sprouting from the tops always made me think of bald men.

The view was familiar. We would head out to Michigan many times during the year, day trips on my father's day off. Going to the country was a treat for me, a city kid. We lived in an apartment in Chicago; all my friends did. But my grandparents owned a home. They had their own backyard. And on top of that, one of my uncles grew corn and had chickens. Once I even saw a chicken running around with his head cut off, a tale I repeated *ad nauseam* to my city friends.

Sometimes we wouldn't stay long. Pa would talk Gramp into going to the track with him. So we would drive the hundred miles back to Chicago, repeating the circuit in the evening. That meant four hundred miles of driving to bet ten races and no time in the country. But I loved those days, too, for at the track I'd be Gramp's secretary.

Before each race, we'd rush down to the paddock, the place where they saddle the horses. Gramp was a comical sight when he hurried. He was a big man whose arms didn't seem to hang right on his body. As he strode next to me, they would dangle as if the puppeteer had cut their strings. He always wore outrageous plaid shirts buttoned up all the way to the neck and his trousers would droop, making it look as if his crotch were a foot lower than it actually was.

Gramp would get up as close to the horses as he could, and screw his face up in concentration. One eye was always half-closed, and he constantly worked his lips as if he were chewing cud. Gramp had no teeth. Actually, he had three sets of teeth, but he always forgot to wear them. They floated in glasses in his bedroom.

"Mark number four in the program," he'd say. "I like his legs. Mark six. He's got good muscles. Seven, too," Gramp would continue. "Make sure you put down seven. Look at the way he carries his head."

Inevitably, he'd wind up marking every horse in the race. Once he finished studying the horses, Gramp would turn to me and ask proudly, "OK, who do I like?"

"Every horse, Gramp. You had me mark every horse in the race."

"Well, that shows it's a hard race to pick. Who does Feldman like? We'll bet with him." He always wound up betting with Feldman, the Jewish handicapper in the *Chicago Sun-Times.*

I watched the dunes rise and fall and rise again as we rolled along but all I could think of was my mother's words. I couldn't imagine Gramp getting old.

When I got to the junkyard, the first person I saw was Norman, the man who worked for my grandfather. He was leaning against the old Ford wrecker, chewing on a toothpick.

"Hi, Norman," I said.

"You don't want to go in there," he replied, pulling the toothpick out of his mouth and pointing it over his shoulder at the office. "You don't want to go in there, Syd."

He was right. When I walked into the small storefront office, my uncle was yelling the same things he'd yelled on the phone. It was if he had been shouting nonstop since he hung up the day before.

As soon as Uncle Jules saw me, he charged out from around the counter, threw his hands in the air, and shouted, "That's it! He's not driving anymore. Last week he hit a tree ten feet off the road. He told me the tree moved." As if he were waiting for an argument, my uncle turned toward my grandfather, who was seated in his favorite green metal rocking chair. But the old man just sat there rocking; he didn't even look up.

"You hear me," my uncle continued, taking the tone of a teacher or parent. He pointed a finger at my grandfather. "No more. Sydney's taking your car. You're not driving anymore." Gramp gave a tiny nod in agreement.

But my uncle wasn't satisfied. He kept shouting and stomping around the small office like a tiny tyrant. My grandfather just sat there looking tired and defeated. I wanted him to do something, to answer my uncle.

Gramp was never shy about saying what was on his mind. When my brother's football team came out to play St. Joe, a nearby town, and got trounced 41-0, he shouted so everyone in the stands could hear, "Bagels! Jewish boys are too full of bagels to play football."

And he wasn't one for subtlety. Once my father asked him to place a bet in a bar that had a secret bookie joint in the back. Pa told him to walk to a door at the right of the bar, knock three times, and ask for Joe. Gramp nodded as if he understood the instructions. But when he walked in, he stopped in the center of the bar and shouted at the bartender, "Where's the bookie joint? I want to place a bet."

I couldn't stand to see him sitting there, taking all that guff from my uncle, so I walked out of the office and back into the junkyard. What I wanted to do was walk back in time, into the junkyard I remembered as a kid. It was a Disneyland of the American automobile. Chryslers, Packards, Pontiacs, Studebakers—every conceivable make and model of car—were piled, stacked, jammed, pushed, crammed, toppled, squashed, and crushed together as far as the eye could see. Some were smashed beyond recognition; others were only slightly crumpled, looking like men who needed their suits pressed. Almost all were missing parts: doors, windshields, trunks. Some, missing tires, wallowed in the mud like pigs. Others rested on their backs like overturned turtles. And still others stood on their tails, or their noses, as if they were circus acrobats.

They created mountains and valleys, plateaus and tunnels, buttes and ravines. I searched through jungles of ripped-out wires, navigated oceans of tires, sneaked through forests of cars piled one on top of the other.

I wanted to walk back in that phantasmagoria of a junkyard and be a kid again. I wanted to jump into the wrecks, pretend I was a driver at the Indy 500, crash, and fall out the window dead. I wanted to walk from the top of one car to the other all the way across the junkyard and then crawl back under the tunnels those same cars created. I wanted to dig behind the seats for matchbooks from strange places or open the glove compartments looking for old love letters. I wanted to chase chickens around the junkyard all morning, and then at lunchtime, crawl out of that hot Michigan sun under a wreck, and just munch on one of the peaches that grew in the corner of the yard.

But as I wandered down one muddy lane after another, I realized that what I really wanted to do was to walk back in the office and find my grandfather king again, the way he was when I was a kid.

The tires piled on each side of the door would look like eight-foot guards. The distributor caps under the window would shine like a pile of jewels. Gramp would stand behind the counter under a canopy of belts and hoses, the wisdom of the ages, the auto parts book spread in front of him.

Gramp always had one answer no matter what you came looking for. As if in deep thought, he would chew on his imaginary cud for awhile. "Do we have it?" he'd finally shrug. "I don't know.

Go in the back and take a look. If we have it, pull it out, bring it up. I'll give you a good price."

What did he know of auto parts? Gramp was a peasant. When you saw him standing next to his wife, they looked as if they were still in the old country. A stocky man, he stood planted as if he were trying to set down roots. He had huge hands and fingers; working man was written all over him. She was almost as heavy as he, a squarish woman, who wore shapeless print dresses that came down to her ankles. She was all chicken soup and matzo balls. He was tough meat.

At my good-bye party for college, he winked at me and waved me toward the kitchen. "Boychick," Gramp said when I got there, "I'm going to tell you the main, important thing you should know before going to college. Sit down."

Gramp turned around, opened the refrigerator, and pulled out two apples. He placed them on a plate and sliced them down the middle. He picked up a half in his big hand and said proudly, "Apples." Gramp winked and nodded sagely, "Apples … the main important thing: put apples in your refrigerator."

At the time I didn't understand the message. I think you'd have to have grown up on the land to understand what he was trying to say. But I did understand the wink. His wink always signaled that what he was saying was important.

One fall he showed up with a station wagon filled with apples. My mother pleaded, "What am I going to do with them?"

Gramp pointed a finger in the air as if he were a rabbi making a point, winked, and announced: "Applesauce."

Another time I was home sick in bed with a cold. He pushed the door open, barged in, and shook me. "Gramp," I asked in a stupor, "What are you doing? I was sleeping."

"I got something for you," he said, sitting down at the edge of my bed. The thought of a present woke me up a little. "I hear you're stuffed up," he continued, reaching into his shirt pocket. "I got something that will open you right up. It's good." Gramp winked and waved a cautionary finger at me. "Don't tell your momma."

It was good and it did open me up. In fact, it brought tears to my eyes. Gramp had poured me a shot of hundred-proof Jack Daniel's.

But the wink I remember best occurred one night when he was sleeping over. Often when he would come into town, he would stay in our apartment, and no matter when I got up, he'd be sitting at the kitchen table, smoking a Pall Mall and staring off into an empty alley. Once I asked him why that was. Gramp smiled, winked, and said, "Old men, we never sleep."

One winter night when he was over, I woke up in the dark. The apartment was freezing because the landlord always turned the heat off around eleven. I looked at my clock and saw that it was 4 A.M. Usually, I would fall right back to sleep—the warmth of the bed was so inviting, my nose was so cold—at least until seven when the heat came back on. Then I would run my clothes out to the living room radiator and hop back in bed for awhile. When I finally did get up, my clothes would be toasty warm.

But on this night I wanted to be up first; I wanted to claim the championship. I thought of sitting there and waiting until he got up, even of putting a Pall Mall in my mouth.

I leaped out of bed, but I came to a dead stop before I reached the kitchen. For a second, I thought I was looking at a ghost. Then I realized it was Gramp, sitting as he always sat, only now in the dark: his sleeves rolled up, ashes falling on his chest, a glass of Jack Daniel's in front of him, an apple on the table. He just sat there, staring off into the dark alley. Gramp never said a word to me as I stood gaping, but from the glow of the tip of the cigarette, I could see his wink.

I wandered through the junkyard for a long time. I didn't want to go back into that office and hear my uncle yelling. I wanted to see that wink again. I threw stones, kicked a can along the dirt road for awhile, even chased a chicken, but finally, I took a deep breath and headed back.

My uncle had finally stopped shouting at my grandfather. Now he was on the phone arguing with a customer. Gramp still sat in the green metal rocker, bobbing slowly up and down. "Hi, Gramp," I said.

He acknowledged me with a small wave of his hand. I didn't know what to do. I wanted to joke with him. I wanted to ask him about the car. I wanted just to talk to him, but I was too frightened to do it. Part of me was scared of what he would say. Then I saw the car keys on the counter. Suddenly, I desperately wanted to leave. I picked the keys up and signaled my uncle. He waved and went back to his conversation. "Gramp, I'm going," I said. Once again, he waved, but he didn't look up.

When I got outside, I took a deep breath. Then I heard the door open behind me. I was surprised to see Gramp. I was embarrassed; I didn't know what to say to him. He motioned me to follow. We moved a short distance from the office. Gramp stopped, his arms swinging awkwardly at his sides, his bad eye half closed. He stared at me. Then he put a finger to his lips and peeked around to see if my uncle had come out of the office. When he saw that we were alone, Gramp turned back to me and winked. "Between you and me, Boychick, that tree did move." Then he smiled for the first time. "Do you know the way to the big road to go home?"

I shook my head no, dumbfounded.

Once again Gramp glanced over his shoulder. "Then follow me," he said. Gramp reached into his shirt pocket and pulled out the keys to the big Ford wrecker. With that, he jumped into the wrecking truck and turned the engine over.

The last scene I remember was a tableau as we pulled away: my uncle running out the office, holding his head and screaming; smoke pouring out of the Ford's exhaust; and Gramp with one hand on the wheel and one hand out the window, waving and winking good-bye.

GRAMP DIED AT SEVENTY-EIGHT. The day he died they took him to the hospital, but they couldn't keep him there. They told him that he couldn't drink and he couldn't smoke. I think he knew that he was going. Gramp went home and called everyone to say good-bye. I talked to him on the phone that last day. He laughed and cried as we talked.

We rushed to Benton Harbor. As we passed the Indiana Dunes, I remembered my earlier trip to pick up his car. I realized that this time he had really gotten old and I hoped we would get there in time.

But we didn't. He had already been taken to the funeral home by the time we arrived. I never got to see him on that last day. But as I stood in the kitchen noticing his Pall Malls and an open bottle of Jack Daniels on the table, I could picture him clearly—smoking, drinking, and winking at God.

A Harvard Man

The radio was blasting, and a cool fall wind whipped through the car. All six of us held beers. One guy beat his can lightly against the car door as he rocked to the music. This wasn't high school where you cruised the neighborhood, screaming out the lyrics of the top forty or yelling pickup lines at clumps of girls as you hung out the car window. This was the first weekend of college and we were heading to our first college party. We wanted to be cool, sophisticated. We wanted to be Harvard men.

How did I come to Harvard? My mother had made it through high school, but my father got thrown out of school in seventh grade. Except for twelve Book-of-the-Month Club selections, the book shelves in our house were filled with knickknacks. We joined the club for one year because my father was a big Capone fan and they were offering *Murder, Inc.* I don't think anyone in the family ever opened the other volumes. There they sat, between a horse rearing up on his hind legs and a smiling Buddha, looking like a treasure that had washed ashore on the wrong island.

When Harvard came recruiting at my high school, I didn't go see the recruiter even though I was a good student. Football claimed my real affection and my college horizon extended only to a small midwestern school where I could play. But my coach, a family friend, made me go see the recruiter at his law office the next week.

"Do you want an education or do you want to play football?" asked the recruiter as soon as I entered.

"An education," I lied.

"Good," he said, "because you probably won't play. You're not prepared for Harvard, and you're going to have to study harder than you can imagine. Sit down and I'll tell you about the college."

How can you say no if Harvard wants you? I sat down in the wood-paneled office and stared out a fifty-fifth story window. The view that stretched for miles made anything seem possible.

But the jump from Albany Park, Chicago, to Cambridge, Massachusetts, wasn't easy. In fact, Harvard totally cowed me that first week.

My first night at dinner I sat with one guy who was composing a symphony and another who had spent his summer hitchhiking around Europe.

The next day I found out that I didn't get into the acting seminar I applied to. I discovered later that a number of the students who had been accepted had been in television series and feature films.

That night, one of my roommates took us home to meet his parents. His father—Harvard '39—led us to a wet bar where, as I watched in amazement, he mixed us each a Bloody Mary.

My father wouldn't have known what a Bloody Mary was; his favorite drink was orange soda. And there certainly wasn't a wet bar in our apartment. We did have a dusty bottle of whiskey in the back of the pantry. It was Seagrams-7 so, as my mother once said when I asked about it, "Someone can have a 7-7 if he wants." I never heard anyone ask for a drink and my parents never offered one. As far as I know, they never opened that bottle.

But it was the first lecture of orientation week that left me wondering what I had gotten myself into. The site of that lecture was Memorial Hall, an imposing fortress of a building. It ran an entire block and stood on its own island, surrounded by streets. Castle-like, Memorial Hall boasted large stained-glass windows and a huge, square clock tower whose clock had burned long ago but had never been replaced. It looked like something from a Dickens novel.

If the outside was ominous, the inside produced a feeling of reverence. When you entered, you stepped into a corridor that was lit by the light filtering through the stained glass. The walls bore patriotic pictures and lists of Harvard men who had died fighting for their country.

The entire freshmen class of one thousand filed silently into Memorial Hall. We were directed to Sanders Theater, a lecture hall that was all dark wood pews and carved beams. This was Harvard: one thousand of us in coats and ties and a professor on a stage in a somber mausoleum of a room. It reeked of tradition.

The lecture flew over my head. When he was done, the lecturer took off his glasses and began to polish them. "Any questions?" he asked.

I stifled a laugh. Questions, I thought. Questions? What freshman could possibly have the courage to ask a question of a Harvard professor in front of a thousand people? They could expel me before I would ever do that. And then a hand shot up not ten feet away from me. The professor nodded in his direction. "Sir …," the student said as he rose. But I never heard the question. I was lost contemplating his ultimate courage and in wondering when I could catch the next bus home.

I know now that we were all in that same boat—insecure, out of place, worried about whether we would make it, wondering why Harvard had chosen us. Even the Eastern prep school crowd, casually cynical and world weary at age eighteen, must have felt insecure that first week.

But then I thought I was alone, a Jew from the Midwest, with three sport coats and one suit that my grandfather had bought me a week earlier. "Labels," he had said to the salesmen. "I only want jackets with good labels on the inside."

Now, on the first weekend in college, I was headed to a party at someone's summer home in the woods. After escaping Boston's tangle of streets and rotaries, we cruised down a winding highway through picturesque stands of trees. I was used to Chicago's corners where the streets met at right angles and huge Midwest expressways that sliced perfect lines through golden corn fields. I gave up trying to figure out where we were headed and concentrated on my Budweiser.

"Who wants another beer back there?" asked one of the guys in the front seat.

The fellow next to me squashed his can in his hand. "I'm ready," he said.

I stared at my can in amazement. I wasn't even at the party and I was already drinking. I had never drunk in high school, not even a beer. In those days the athletes were straight, at least at my school. No cigarettes, no booze.

I drained the last few swallows. "Me, too," I smiled, squashing my can. I felt great.

The summer home was tucked neatly between two oak trees in a clearing in the woods. As I sauntered in, I surveyed the scene: the music was blasting, the place was jammed, some couples were making out on a nearby couch. A black guy stood next to the stereo, rocking to the music. He held his arm straight out in front of him, his hand balled up into a fist. When he saw that I was puzzled, he smiled and said, "I'm holding the bag, and I'm about to let the cat out." With that, he opened his fist and danced off into the crowd.

An earnest looking fellow approached and shot a hand out. "Hi, I'm Bob," he said. "Drinks are that-a-way, in the kitchen." Then, before I could even reply, he moved on like a politician to meet other guests.

As I headed toward the kitchen, I checked out the girls. I was astounded; none wore white socks. In my high school the good girls always wore white socks, usually with gym shoes. It was a badge of virginity: white = purity; gym shoes = wholesome activity. The bad girls' legs were bare or covered in nylons and they wore flats.

There was something about bare legs. In high school I found it hard to concentrate as I followed their naked promise to where they disappeared under a skirt. Ah, to sail to that mystical port.

But those bare-legged high school girls were forbidden fruit. My crew of guys never really made passes at them. We left that for the greasers. We were the good guys. We wore white T-shirts under our regular shirts and sported crew cuts. We couldn't be seen talking to bad girls in the school hallway because everyone would know what was on our minds. Of course, that was ironic because sex was on everyone's mind.

Once I did make friends with a bad girl. Fate had made us lab partners in a science class. She was fun to talk to. She told me that every weekend she danced on what was Chicago's equivalent of *American Bandstand.* The next Saturday I watched her on television: tight skirt, bare-legged, smiling, sexy, wild. She danced through my dreams for many nights after that. I think she wanted me to take her to the dance show but I never did. She was a Capulet and I was a Montague.

But at this party every girl had bare legs or wore nylons. There wasn't a white sock in the place, and none of the guys wore white T-shirts. Not even me. It wasn't the style at Harvard, so my chest hair was seeing the light of day for the first time. I felt like James Dean in a crew cut, adrift in the sophistication of bare legs, exposed chests, and drinks.

"Scotch?" asked a smiling preppie type in a blazer, when I

reached the kitchen. He held up a bottle.

"That's fine," I replied. It became my standard answer. "Gin? That's fine." (It tasted like hair tonic.) "Tequila? That's fine." (Who could taste it after the salt?) "Vodka? That's fine." (Completely tasteless.) "Wine? That's fine." (You call this a drink?)

I worked my way through the liquor as if it were a Whitman Sampler. I didn't know that you shouldn't mix drinks. I also didn't know that you shouldn't drink quickly. I was really chugging them. All I knew was that I was enjoying myself at a college party and that my fears about fitting in were disappearing.

But soon everything began to spin, even when I kept my eyes closed. Couples, furniture, woods, all seemed to be caught up in a whirlpool. People loomed in and out of my vision. I caught glimpses of legs, breasts, eyes. Two guys with broad grins asked if I wanted another drink and then disappeared. All I wanted was to find my roommate, Dave, so he could take me home. The problem was that I couldn't focus on people's faces.

I stumbled into someone and placed a hand on his shoulder, hoping to keep him steady. "Do you know where Dave is?" I asked.

"Dave who?" he replied, filled with real concern. I couldn't explain and so I just patted his chest and moved on.

At some point I made my way out of the house and began to wander through the woods. The cool air and the quiet felt good. I'm not sure how long I walked before I tripped and landed in a patch of leaves and dirt. I rolled over on my back to have a talk with God. I was feeling very sick; in fact, I was sure I was going to die.

"Please, God," I pleaded, "save me. I promise I'll never drink again if you just save my life." I was ready to promise anything. If there had been the Jewish equivalent of an order of monks, I would have vowed to join it.

Just then I heard voices. I was hoping that it was Dave and the guys I came with, but it was a couple from the party. They were walking straight toward me. "Oh baby … oh baby," the guy murmured as he kissed the girl and ran a hand over her breast.

"Yes, John, oh yes … yes," she replied, as she fumbled at the buttons of his shirt. They were walking and kissing and talking and getting out of their clothes all at once. I was amazed. It seemed like some challenge you might see on *Beat the Clock.*

The girl spread a blanket on the grass not thirty feet away from me. They lay down, removed the final pieces of their clothing, and began to make love. I remembered wondering why they weren't cold, and whether one could throw up noiselessly. So there we were like some scene in a movie: the two of them naked on a blanket, getting hotter and hotter, and me in the dirt getting sicker and sicker.

John: "Oh, baby, yes …."
Me: "Oh, God, no …."
John: "Oh, baby, yes, yes …."
Me: "Oh, God, no no …."
John: "Oh, baby, baby …."
Me: "Oh, God, God …."
John: "YES … YES!"
Me: "NO … NO!"
John: "OH … OH!"
Me: "UH … OH!"

I stood then. There really wasn't anything to say to make it better. I tried to be as polite as possible. "Please excuse me," I said. I then shrugged my shoulders and began vomiting.

I'll never forget their looks: part fear, part anger, part wonder, part disgust. It was as if I were some mythical monster sent by their parents. They were speechless.

I staggered past them into the woods. As I wandered off, they stayed locked together, watching me in wordless disbelief.

I passed out a little later. I no longer cared about being sophisticated, about being accepted, about the poor couple, about my roommate. All I wanted to do was sleep. I curled up in a ball beneath a pretty birch tree. I tried to cover myself with leaves.

That's where my friends found me hours later. The next day I heard that they had sent search parties out to look for me in the woods. My roommate carried me back to the car. My head was still a jumble and they had to stop the car several times on the way home to let me puke.

I threw up for the last time at one of the gates leading into Harvard yard, the one right in front of Massachusetts Hall, a building that had quartered the Continental Army.

Welcome to college. Welcome to sophistication. I was a Harvard man.

Harvard Man Redux

By my sophomore year at Harvard I felt as if I belonged. With five roommates, I moved into a sprawling four-bedroom suite on the top floor of Leverett House. The room's gabled eaves made it look like something out of a novel.

My life began to seem like a novel, too. I'd closed the chapter on the Jewish kid growing up in Albany Park, Chicago, and had opened a sophisticated new one, containing weekly get-togethers with the headmaster over sherry, glee club concerts, and the Harvard marching band parading through the square on football Saturday mornings. I had become a Harvard man, part of the landscape that had once been Emerson's, Thoreau's, and J.F.K.'s.

Imitating my professors, I strode through Harvard yard on blustery days with only a sport coat for protection. I even made sure my tie blew casually over one shoulder in the wind. I participated in tortured philosophical discussions at the Blue Parrot—a sixties basement coffee house where you could sip espresso to Bach's *Brandenburg Concertos.* I wrote endless free verse on the banks of the Charles River. In other words, I had become completely sophomoric.

My newfound confidence translated itself into a sophisticated disdain for my courses. I had signed up for History of the South, a course contemptuous former students labeled Mint Julep. My second-year Italian course covered Dante's *Inferno,* a work I figured

I could always skim in translation. English 10 surveyed the entire history of English literature, but in my new frame of mind, I relished playing the role of literary dilettante. A course I took to fulfill a social studies requirement, Constitutional Law, even sounded as if it just might be interesting.

The large class assembled in Sanders Theater, scene of my freshman orientation meetings. A professor from the law school strode to the podium. With his bald head, bow tie, and tweed sport coat, he looked as if he'd answered a casting call for a professorial type.

He beamed at us that first morning. "Ladies and gentlemen," he began, "I'm going to run this class as I would a law school course. That means I expect you to be prepared every day. On your way out, you can pick up a syllabus of the required readings." I didn't hear much of the rest of his introduction because I was pondering this novel idea: be prepared for class, every day.

"Hey," I wanted to say, "I'm a Harvard man. My time is my own. I go to class when I want, study when I want, and cram like mad when I have to." But I was worried. I knew that the class would contain many fledgling lawyers who would actually do the reading.

The following day the professor opened class by posing a long, hypothetical question, rich in nuance and fraught with implications. The question concerned a constitutional issue that the dutiful students had undoubtedly read about the night before.

Then the professor pulled a class list from his briefcase and placed it on the podium. "Adams, John," he called out and peered over the top of his reading glasses. He waited. And waited. And waited. Because even if John Adams was there, he wasn't about to admit it.

"It seems Mr. Adams is not with us this morning," the professor finally said. "So let us hear from … Mr. James Hertel."

Not only was Hertel inexplicably absent, but the next eight

names he called weren't present either. On the next try, he landed on me. Without even blinking, I stared straight ahead. A friend next to me bit his lip to keep from laughing.

Finally, the professor resorted to a more direct means of instigating some intellectual give and take. "You there, in the blue shirt," he said, intently peering over his glasses at a particular individual directly in front of him, "please stand and answer the question."

But the fellow in the blue shirt looked from side to side as if he thought his shirt might have turned white. I'm sure he hoped that some poor blue-shirted sucker in the vicinity would stand.

"You," shouted the professor, pointing directly at him. "You, right there."

Disingenuously, the student pointed at himself and mouthed, "Me?"

"Yes, you!" roared the professor.

The student stood. "Can you repeat the question, sir?" he asked.

The professor braced himself by holding unto the podium. He paused for a long time, trying to maintain his composure. Finally, he took a deep breath and repeated the question.

"Sorry sir, but I didn't do the reading," said the student and sat down.

Each day the professor's smile lost some of its beam, and the corners of his mouth began to sag until his face was infused with sadness. Occasionally, he would luckily land on a potential law school student eager to answer his question, but more often than not he'd choose an irresponsible undergraduate, taking the course just to fulfill a requirement.

It soon got around that if you came early, you could sneak into the Sanders balcony and lie on the floor. That way you could take notes and avoid the embarrassment of being called on. So each day the visible class shrank. People must have thought the course was one of the most popular in the university because students would line up early waiting for the doors to open. By late October the balcony was wall-to-wall students. It looked like a weird sleep-over where you were required to wear ties and take notes.

As the fall progressed, I donned a scarf, which now blew over my shoulder along with my tie, and continued to stride thoughtlessly through the year.

I had other things to do besides study. For one thing, I was so nervous freshman year that I hadn't explored Boston, especially the North End. So I began to spend long weekend afternoons there, soaking up the Italian atmosphere as I wandered through the fruit and vegetable markets. Or I'd hide myself away in Harvard's Lamont Library, listening to the records in their poetry collection. And who had time to study at night? Over a jug of cheap wine, I much preferred discussing life with my friends.

In early November I had to write four research papers in twenty-four hours. Not surprisingly, I netted three D's and an F. Midterm exams loomed up like evil demons on the horizon.

For all I knew, the South could have been a foreign country. In Italian I found myself lost in Purgatory. More and more I drifted off to sleep on the Sanders' balcony floor. And as my survey course rushed us through centuries of English literature, I fell further and further behind.

By the time I decided to study, I was so far behind my efforts could make little difference. English was typical. Very late the night before the exam, my roommate Jay and I tested each other with spot quotes from the literature. We had each done about half the required work. At three a.m. we called it quits when I read Jay the ingredients off a box of Kellogg's Corn Flakes and he guessed that the list was what Gulliver had packed for his travels.

The next morning Jay woke me up from a fretful four-hour

sleep and led me into our common room where he had created a running track by rearranging our furniture. He had also thrown open the windows so the freezing air would wake us up. As I ran, I knew that even though my mind might be awake, it was still woefully empty.

Midterm exams proved to be my comeuppance. I felt like Robert E. Lee after Mint Julep was over. Italian contained a long translation of a passage that I swore was neither in Heaven nor Hell, let alone Purgatory. A major question in Constitutional Law featured material that I must have snoozed through. And I was forced to use the shotgun approach in English. That's when you throw yourself on the mercy of your grader by writing everything you know about the course because you don't know anything about the question.

At Christmas break, I arranged to drive someone's car to Grand Rapids, Michigan, where my father agreed to pick me up even though it was 180 miles from Chicago. I thought a spell of being alone on the highway would help me lick my wounds.

Indeed, the further away I got from Cambridge, the better I felt. Passing through the rocky landscape of western Massachusetts, the courses and the exams no longer seemed so important. By the Berkshires my confidence had bounded back. In mid-New York state I began to sing Harvard fight songs:

Resistless our team sweeps goalward
With the fury of the blast.
We'll fight for the name of Harvard
Till the last white line is passed.

The songs roused me. By Rochester I changed into a Harvard sweatshirt, hoping to impress people at rest stops.

Somewhere around Buffalo I made a fateful choice. I could have followed the interstate as it swung south past Lake Erie, then headed back north to Grand Rapids. Instead I chose to leave the interstate and proceed into Canada, passing through Ontario and heading directly to my destination.

"Canada it is," I said. Now this wouldn't have been a bad choice if my radio had been working, if I hadn't had been driving all day, if the road weren't a poorly lighted two-lane highway, and if it hadn't started snowing.

I knew that I should pull off when I found myself fighting to keep my eyes open. But like the teams in the Harvard fight songs, I struggled on. I opened the window, slapped my cheeks, and tried to sing the complete score of *West Side Story.*

In the middle of "Tonight," I fell asleep. The next thing I knew, my foot was on the brake, my hands were frozen to the steering wheel, and my heart sounded louder than the motor. Luckily, I landed safely in a field.

I berated myself as I backed the car onto the road: How dumb can you be? I thought. I was about to get the answer.

I stopped at the first motel I saw. Still angry with myself, I parked and walked toward what looked like a small home. The home served as the office for about a half dozen small units behind it.

My hand was on the doorknob when it suddenly occurred to me that I had no idea whether they spoke English or French in Ontario.

I stood there looking at my chagrined reflection in the window of the front door. "Harvard" appeared written backwards across my chest, taunting me. Perfect, I thought. I know who is housed on the third ring of Hell. I can tell you the rhyme scheme of a Shakespearean sonnet. I can explain Louis Nizer's position on a number of constitutional issues. And I can expound on the effect the carpetbaggers had on the South. But I don't know whether they speak English in Ontario.

Sheepishly I entered a small room that contained an old-fashioned roll-top desk, a couch, an overstuffed chair, and a coffee table. Little knickknacks, mostly animals, were sprinkled about, and plants lined the windows. I searched for something written—a calendar, an ad—but nothing appeared to rescue me from my dilemma.

In the soft chair sat a grandmotherly woman in bifocals, who wore a sweater over her shoulders. A book rested on her lap. She gave me a kind smile when I entered.

I panicked as she patiently waited for me to say something. I tried to think of any French I knew. I remembered the nursery rhyme, "Frere Jacques." It contained the phrase *dormez-vous*, and I considered singing the rhyme to her.

Why it didn't occur to me to speak in English or to simply ask if she spoke English I'll never know. This was Ontario, not rural France. Even if she spoke French, she would have been used to English from television and radio. And after all, she was running a business for travelers. But none of these thoughts passed through this Harvard man's mind.

She looked puzzled. Obviously, I was struggling with some problem. I knew I had to do something, so finally, Tonto-like, I blurted out, "Me want sleep." To make matters worse, I mimicked the action by putting my hands together and resting my head on them. The woman was nonplussed. "Bed," I said and then pointed at myself.

She sat there for the longest time with a quizzical look on her face and then in a beautifully articulated voice with a delightful English accent, she asked, "Are you looking for a motel room?"

I snapped straight up, trying to be cool. "Yes, a room." I laughed as if it were all a joke. "Yes, a room for the night. That's what I want. A room."

She handed me a form but eyed me suspiciously the whole

time I was signing in. I'm sure she thought I was psychotic. The next day I paid without looking up and left hurriedly.

I desperately wanted to get home. I didn't want to impress anyone anymore. Most of the day I pushed through a snowstorm and arrived in Grand Rapids a little later than I had hoped. I dropped the car off and headed by taxi to the bus depot, where I had arranged to meet my parents.

The first person I saw was my uncle. He was pacing up and down, an unlit cigar tucked in the corner of his mouth. I was happy that he had come along to meet me.

"Uncle Itchky," I yelled, waving wildly.

He looked up without a smile, glowering with his hands on his hips as I crossed toward him. "What's wrong?" I asked.

"What's wrong?" he repeated. He raised his eyes to the heavens as if he were proving to God how dumb I was. "What's wrong?" he asked the sky.

He pulled the cigar out of his mouth and pointed it at me. "I'll tell what's wrong. You're what's wrong! How can you ask your father to drive through a blizzard to get you? We came through a goddamn blizzard. Sixteen-wheelers were running off the road. I kept telling your father to turn around, but no, he had to pick you up. He drove the goddamn car into a snowbank and we had to be towed out. But did that stop him? No. He had to get you."

"I didn't know about the storm," I whined.

"Enough already," said my father who had walked up during the tirade. "Let's get going. It's going to be a long ride home."

But Uncle Itchky wasn't finished. He muttered to himself as we walked to the car, occasionally throwing his arms into the air as if to prove a point.

All the way back to Benton Harbor where we were going to drop Itchky off, he talked. Every time he saw a jackknifed truck, he pointed it out. Every car buried in the snow was grist for his mill.

Like belches, phrases kept popping out of him: "Sure, he thinks he's smart ... Big deal college student ... Harvard man ... No brains."

I was sitting in the back seat with my mother. She waved her hand the first time Itchky said something, indicating I shouldn't pay any attention. "You know the Liebermans," she whispered. "They're always yelling." Then she slipped me a tuna fish sandwich she had made for me. "You must be hungry," she said.

I sank deeper into my seat, feeling more and more childlike, and less and less like a Harvard man. I must have fallen asleep because when I woke up we were somewhere south of the Loop. "Are we almost home?" I asked instinctively. It's what I always used to say when I was little and we were heading home from a trip.

"No dear, go back to sleep," my mother replied. "We'll be home soon."

As she smoothed my hair with her hand, it occurred to me that I wouldn't have to worry about final exams for another month. I closed my eyes and peacefully drifted off to sleep.

Love and Lust

As long as I can remember, I yearned for love. I had a girlfriend by the time I was in second grade. While other guys played marbles, I played jacks. Some nights I would sneak out to stand in front of Elyse's apartment building and gaze at her brightly lit windows. One night it began to snow softly while I stood there. I was so overwhelmed by emotion that I began to sing "Silent Night."

At age fourteen I fell in love for real. I met Adrienne in the library. I had gone there with my pal Richard Kuznitsky to look for a book on David Livingston, the explorer. Adrienne was there with her friend, Judy Immergluck.

Rich and I were sitting at a little table in the children's room. We had sought refuge from the snarling librarian with pince-nez glasses who prowled the adult section. The children's room held a special meaning for me. My grandmother had taken me there to pick out my first book, *The Five Chinese Brothers.* In the book each brother is saved from death because he can do something miraculous: drink an ocean, hold his breath as long as he wants, withstand fire, etc.

I didn't expect a miracle to happen to me that day, but one did. I fell in love at first sight. Adrienne sat at a table near the window, looking like a combination of Jackie Kennedy, Audrey Hepburn, and Annette Funicello. As soon as I saw her, I felt like a sixth brother, capable of anything. Love can do that to you.

I looked at Adrienne and she looked back. I swear she winked and that's why I went over, but she has always denied it. She maintains that she was just admiring my club jacket.

I was flaunting a blue and orange Condor jacket that a high school senior had lent me until I could buy my own. In those days in our neighborhood, we had clubs. I had just been accepted into a popular club called the Condors. It didn't matter that the jacket was two sizes too big for me and bore several large stains. My Condor jacket was proof that I was cool. I approached Adrienne's table feeling like a knight in a fairy tale, wearing magic armor. It didn't hurt either that I was a high school freshman while she was an eighth grader.

A few weeks later, Judy Immergluck invited me to a New Year's Eve party at her house. Of course, Adrienne was going to be there. The party teetered on the edge of adolescence. There were popcorn fights, girls rushing off to the bathroom together, and clumps of boys feeling a little bit like settlers surrounded by a swirling band of Indians. The mellow music of Johnny Mathis surrounded us as Adrienne and I slow-danced in a darkened living room, held hands in shadowy dark corners, and played spin the bottle.

Spin the bottle: the game of fate. It must have been fate, because when I spun the Coke bottle, it pointed directly at Adrienne.

In subsequent years, kisses would just be a point of departure, the warm-up act, the appetizer. But not this kiss; this was a real kiss, a first kiss. This kiss consummated our fledgling relationship. As our lips parted and our minty breaths mingled, I was filled with the ache of excitement and longing. I felt puzzled and surprised and happy and sad all at once, just as a tadpole must feel as it becomes a frog, or a caterpillar must feel right before it emerges from its cocoon.

At 1 A.M., I walked home in a daze. I stopped in the center of the snow-filled high school campus that stretched for two blocks, looked up at the clear sky filled with bright stars, and began to sing and dance à la Gene Kelly,

"I'm singing in the snow,
just singing in the snow.
What a glorious feeling,
I'm hap-hap-happy, you know."

Ah, I was crazy in love.

I loved Adrienne the only way a fourteen-year-old boy can love a girl: schizophrenically. Sometimes I didn't know what to say to her. As my tongue lay heavy in my mouth, I frantically searched for subjects that would interest her. At other times I'd take the phone into my bedroom, lie on my bed, and for hours talk to her about nothing.

We celebrated Adrienne's graduation from eighth grade by going to downtown Chicago. We ate at Henrici's and saw *A Hole in the Head* at the State and Lake Theater. She wore a navy blue sailor jumper. It rained. We stared into each other's eyes and ate soggy popcorn on the way home.

I spent my days in a haze of longing for her. I would even go out of my way to walk by her house just in case she happened to come out. I was living the song, "On the Street Where You Live."

Of course, a kiss soon lost its importance. It might have been fine for a Knight of the Round Table, but in real life the sap was rising in our little bodies, and so, along with Ann Landers, we had to consider the eternal issue of necking and petting and how far to go.

It wasn't very far. The only place we could make out was at the Terminal Theater on Friday nights. No synagogue for us. We were praying for other things.

Now you could flirt all you wanted in the center of the theater, toss popcorn at the girls to get their attention, lean over their shoulders and sip their Cokes through a straw, but if you wanted to do some serious making out, you headed over to the couples' corner, several rows at the edge of the theater set aside for the real thing.

The problem was that a number of girls cruised up and down the aisles in this section to see who was with whom, and more importantly, who was doing what with whom. Some of Adrienne's friends were among the cruisers.

On some Friday nights we gave in to our desires and provided the original information highway with something to report. We necked our way through entire films and woke up Saturday with sore lips. At other times, Adrienne's righteous upbringing took over and we would have long talks about how I should appreciate her more for her mind than her body.

Of course, it couldn't last. We were together too much and I needed to be with the guys. I'd hear tales of the baseball games I had missed or the fun my friends had had at Nick's Pizza joint, seeing how long they could stretch a piece of cheese.

After we broke up, we didn't speak, even avoiding saying hello in the high school hallways. And then a year after I got into Harvard, Adrienne got into Radcliffe. The summer before she began, Adrienne invited me over to her house to tell her about college. Immediately, I fell in love with her all over again.

There was just one problem. She already had a boyfriend. So I became her friend and advisor. Talk about the fox guarding the henhouse. The first bit of advice I gave her was to dump the boyfriend.

After she took my advice, I began to major in Adrienne. Sophomore year I almost flunked out of school because of her. I wrote Adrienne an epic poem that took thirty minutes to recite.

The opus was filled with melodramatic lines like these:

we stood there facing each other
and while the chandeliers crashed
and the mirrors cracked
and while the music screamed
I touched your hair

Now that we were older, the issue of what to do about sex bubbled and boiled constantly between us. We still had the motive and now we had the opportunity. One would think we would have done the deed. But we didn't. Adrienne and I would spend long evenings in my dorm room with Ravel's "Afternoon of a Faun" on the record player for mood. We'd eat grapes and cheese and bread and drink wine—I had just read Omar Khayyam—and we'd neck and pet but only go so far.

No doubt that sounds odd or terribly old-fashioned to young people today, but they don't understand the ambiance of our sexual world in the late fifties and early sixties. I can describe it in two words: Doris Day. The Age of Doris Day preceded the sexual revolution. In all her movies Doris's leading man wanted to do it and sometimes she even wanted to do it, but they never did. They talked about it and they teased about it, but until wedding bells rang in technicolor, they remained pure. You might have wanted to, you might have been driven crazy by desire, but in the Age of Doris Day you just weren't supposed to do it with a good girl. Even the *Playboys* that I sneaked into my house reinforced this notion. Their sexy centerfolds featured girl-next-door-types. You saw the girls' breasts, but the rest was off limits. You could even imagine bringing one of those wholesome *Playboy* girls home to meet your mother.

My friends and I always dated good girls and hoped to run into a bad one. We all had permanent rings worn into our wallets from the rubbers we carried there just in case we got lucky.

It was an age of yearning, of unconsummated relationships and sexual tension. In a perverse way, we came to treasure it. The Everly Brothers sang what could have been the age's theme song:

Dre-e-e-e-eam, dream, dream, dream,
Dre-e-e-e-eam, dream, dream, dream,
When I want you in my arms,
When I want you and all your charms,
Whenever I want you, all I have to do is
Dre-e-e-e-eam, dream, dream, dream.

Yes, we could dream about it, but we weren't supposed to do it. Yet it wasn't easy controlling our seething hormones, especially when one day the perfect opportunity presented itself.

My father sat in his favorite position, in front of the television set with his pants off. His belly hung over his boxer shorts, making him look like Buddha in underwear. "Hey Root," he yelled to my mother, Ruth, in the kitchen. "Let's go visit my parents tomorrow on my day off. We'll sleep over in Benton Harbor and come back on Thursday."

"But what about Sydney?" she yelled back over the sound of running water. "He's got a summer job. He can't go."

"He'll be all right," Pa yelled.

"Sure I will," I added, but my thoughts were elsewhere. Words were flashing in my mind like the neon lights on a marque: Adrienne! All Night! Adrienne! All Night! Adrienne! All Night!

My mother walked into the living room, wiping her hands on a dish towel. "You have to remember to close all the windows and lock all the doors," she said. "And don't forget to check the gas." The last item was something she always did when leaving, sometimes more than once.

"Sure, he'll remember," said my father, "he's a Harvard student." He turned toward me with a smile. "You can remember, can't you?"

Adrienne and I began Thursday evening at Nick's. It had been the local pizza joint until Nick added on a room with tables, checkerboard tablecloths, and candles in little red glass bowls. Now he called the place Nick's Ristorante.

We could have been on a first date. Over a stringy, oily thin crust pizza (the real Chicago pizza), we once again found ourselves tongue-tied. We sat there silently staring into each other's eyes, while in the other room Nick yelled at a new generation of teens, "Hey, if you don't stop horsing around, I'm going to throw you out." We felt very sophisticated, especially because in the back of both of our minds, we were thinking about where we were headed.

We entered the apartment like a giggly, young married couple. I even carried her over the threshold. The place was ours. We could do whatever we wanted. My instinctive reaction was to head for the kitchen and see what there was to eat. But I fought down that impulse along with the one that told me to turn on the T.V.

We sat in the living room on my parents' plastic-covered couch and made awkward small talk for awhile.

"Comfortable?" I asked.

"Yes."

"Want anything?"

"No."

"Oh."

The sound of crinkling plastic filled the long silences. We both knew where we wanted to go and what we wanted to do, but neither of us wanted to seem too anxious.

I had also begun to feel a little tentative. The open door to my bedroom yawned before me, and I suddenly realized that I was going to bring a girl into my bedroom and my boyhood bed. I was going to desecrate with lust the inner sanctum of my boyhood.

When we first moved in, I had picked the wallpaper for the

bedroom: boy wallpaper with drawings of trophies and different sporting equipment on it. My boy wastebasket was laminated with a collage of college pennants.

Growing up, my brother and I had shared this room, doing boy things. We played basketball, tossing a tennis ball through a basket made up of a twisted hanger stuck into a closed closet door. We shot down pigeons and sparrows with our fingers, pretending to be pilots shooting down bombers and fighters. We wrestled there. We fought there. The only time he'd ever really socked me with a fist was in that bedroom.

I even learned how real men decided things there. My brother's bed was placed in front of the room's only window, while mine was tucked into a dark corner. In the summer, that dark corner got really hot, and so one night I asked my brother why he always got the bed by the window. He raised his head off the pillow and said, "Because, I'm bigger and tougher." Then he rolled over and went to sleep.

And now I was contemplating bringing Adrienne into this shrine of boyhood, this repository of machismo, this anvil of masculinity, and for what? Sex.

"Let's go to bed," she said.

"Sure," I replied, her words canceling all my concerns. Women can do that to you. One minute you're out with the guys scarfing down popcorn and guzzling beer at a football game, and the next minute you abandon them happily to sip post-symphony tea with a girl.

We necked. We petted. We were lost in clouds of billowing clothes, made breathless by the thought of what was to come. The night was all naked skin and darkness. And the night was long. To hell with good girls and bad girls. To hell with the rules. To hell with Doris Day.

Then suddenly we froze. We heard voices at the front door.

Adrienne's eyes grew as big as a spotlighted deer's. I heard a key being turned in the lock. The door opened. "Get me something to eat, Root," boomed my father. "I'm dead tired, but I'm glad we came back tonight instead of sleeping there."

"What do you want? A cheese sandwich?" asked my mother.

"Let's get dressed," Adrienne whispered.

"Let's wait," I replied. "Maybe they'll go to bed after my father eats."

As if on cue, my father said, "Let's watch some T.V." We both grimaced.

The laugh track we heard when the television came on fit the moment. I was about to suggest that we get dressed while the television was on. I figured we could always say we were sleeping when the television woke us up. Then I heard my mother say, "I wonder if Sydney closed the window in his bedroom?" We stared at each other, wondering if we could get all our clothes on, make the bed, and pretend we were reading before she entered. I thought of throwing the blanket over us but I knew that wouldn't work. We were trapped.

We could hear her walking toward the room. Then the door opened and she stuck in her head. Noticing clothes strewn all over the floor, she started to do her motherly cleaning thing. Then she saw us: her baby naked in bed, holding a naked girl in his arms. I didn't know what she would do: start screaming, start crying, faint, go into shock. Experts say that at moments of stress we rely on our basic instincts: fighters fight, fleers flee. Well, my Jewish mother proved the rule.

"You want a tuna fish sandwich?" she asked. Then she closed the door and we got dressed in silence. Sheepishly we came out and chatted with my parents for a few minutes before I drove Adrienne home. Neither of us could swallow a bite.

So Adrienne and I had to wait a little longer to make love. I'm happy to report that eventually we did, and the act lived up to my expectations. Now, thirty years later, after twenty-eight years of marriage, a lot has changed in out relationship, but we still choose sex over sandwiches, and we usually lock the door.

The Real Africa

By eight in the morning the temperature had topped ninety degrees. I was sunk in a hammock on my porch, mesmerized by a woman's rhythmic chant as she beat the husks off rice. Then I heard a Land Rover pull off the highway and begin bumping its way down the dirt road to my house. It had to be Joe.

As soon as he saw me, he began to beep and wave. At the sound, kids came running. Some adults, hoping to be entertained, stepped out of their houses to see what the commotion was about. The last time Joe had come to the village, I was with him. After we roared to a stop, we climbed up on top of the Land Rover and sang "America the Beautiful" to my frowning wife and about fifty hysterical villagers.

"Syd, let's go," Joe yelled as he pulled up. "This is it! I'm finally going to get my chance." He beeped the horn several times as if it were a drum. "I'm finally going to have my adventure. Tell your wife you'll be back late tonight or tomorrow morning. Come on!" Because it was Joe, I didn't even ask where we were going.

He was from New York City and I was from Chicago and that was our bond. It didn't matter that he was Irish and I was Jewish, that he was in his late thirties and I was in my middle twenties, that he was the head of the teaching program and I was just a teacher in it. We were big city boys who talked with our hands and said "dis" and "dat." And even though our accents were different, they were heavy.

We were five thousand miles from home, in Sierra Leone, West Africa, in the Peace Corps. It was 1969, the tail end of the real Peace Corps, the J.F.K. Ask-What-You-Can-Do-For-Your-Country Peace Corps when any red-blooded American thought he could teach a native how to do something better than the native had been doing it all of his life.

I went over as a farmer. I was going to teach African farmers how to grow rice in swamps, a perfect job for a Chicago boy. Not only had I never seen a swamp, I had never been on a farm. I had never planted anything, not even a tomato plant. The apartment building where I grew up didn't have a backyard. I couldn't pick a rice plant out of a lineup, but I had the best of intentions.

We gathered in Philadelphia to hear lectures about what to expect and what we shouldn't do: get high on marijuana. We also got our teeth fixed. In 1969 dentistry in Sierra Leone was primitive. But they didn't do so well in Philadelphia either. I'll never forget the look on a friend's swollen face as the Novocaine wore off and he rolled his tongue over the two wisdom teeth that had just been pulled. He stopped in mid-roll and looked quizzically at me. "Syd," he said slowly, "they yanked the wrong teeth." He had to go back the next day to get the right ones pulled.

And so with great expectations, high ideals, and sound teeth—the ones that were left—we took off for West Africa. In Philadelphia they told us that Sierra Leone was in the "armpit of Africa." This metaphor turned out to refer to heat more than to the location. If you picture the continent as a man saluting you, Sierra Leone would be just below his elbow.

We flew to Madrid first, then refueled and headed south, flying for hours over the Sahara desert. And then, just when I had given up hope of seeing anything but sand, rain clouds billowed up all around us. The world turned green, and winding rivers, like huge snakes, seemed to twist everywhere. We had arrived in tropical Africa.

Adrienne and I looked at each other with excitement. We had chucked good jobs for the adventure of experiencing life in West Africa. And there it lay below us.

Stepping off the plane was like stepping onto the pages of *National Geographic.* Jungle crept right up to the field, and bare-breasted women with baskets on their heads walked right onto the runway, waiting to sell us peanuts. The heat hit us immediately, a humid, sticky, heavy heat that even Chicago summers hadn't prepared us for.

When we entered the terminal, two old volunteers greeted us. They were wearing sweaters and cheerfully explained that this was the rainy season, or the cool time of year. We sprawled all over the terminal—exhausted from the trip and the heat—and waited for the director to show up.

Then one new volunteer began to scream. She had opened her box of homemade chocolate chip cookies to discover that they were swarming with ants. The seasoned volunteers smiled knowingly at each other. One reached over, took a cookie covered with ants, gave it a casual swipe, and popped it into his mouth. "It doesn't matter if you get them all," he said as he reached for another. "They're good protein." On the spot, one couple decided to return home.

We were sent up-country to a college at Njala for training in language and farming. In the morning we sat in language class with our pants open. Fanning our private parts, we tried to get rid of our crotch rot as we struggled with the Mende, the tribal language of the region. Mende's a tonal language in which the same word might mean snake or rope or stick depending on the tone in which it is said. One day my instructor gave me a puzzled look and asked, "Why did you say, 'Are your pants on fire?' " I had been trying to say, "Are you cooking dinner?"

In the afternoons, they trained us to be swamp farmers. At least that's what they said they were doing. It turned out that the Agricultural Department, which was in charge of our training, saw this as a chance to gain publicity. So our training largely consisted of photo opportunities.

They would drive us to a village where we would file onto the chief's front porch. There we would sit in a long line, facing the chief and the village elders. They would smile and nod a lot. We would smile and nod a lot. More times than not someone would pass Cokes to everyone, and we would all hold them up and smile and nod some more. Then we would drink our Cokes, shake hands, and leave. It might have made a great commercial, but it wasn't training.

When they finally took us to a farm, it wasn't even a swamp farm, but a hillside rice farm. We didn't actually get to see much of it. It seems we had unwittingly crushed the farmer's ginger, his money crop, as we crossed the field. The furious farmer chased us off with a machete.

The day they finally took us to a swamp was the day my training as a farmer ended. We hiked five miles through the jungle. The temperature was close to one hundred, and for most of the trek it rained. The deluge became so heavy at times that I couldn't see past the edge of my umbrella.

The swamp was surrounded by jungle. Birds chattered; monkeys screeched. I kept expecting a lion to crash through the trees and attack us. Oblivious to it all, the veteran volunteer in a Chinese coolie hat slogged knee-deep in mud. We crowded around him in the swamp and watched him plant rice for an hour. The whole time I kept thinking of the moment in *The Wizard of Oz* when Dorothy left the world of black and white and stepped into the color of Munchkinland. She looked at her dog and said, "Toto, I have a feeling we're not in Kansas anymore."

I left the swamp scene that day and joined the teaching program. I'd been a teacher for two years, and I knew much more about teaching than I knew about farming. In the teaching program, I met Joe.

Joe had been a highly paid educational consultant in New York, but his desire for adventure led him to join the Peace Corps. To his dismay, the Peace Corps parked him in an administrative position in Freetown, the capital of Sierra Leone. Freetown was the New York City of the country. It came complete with pollution, crowds, traffic jams, and even big city thieves.

Those thieves were a special breed. They had seen a lot of American cowboy movies, so gangs roamed the city like rustlers, not on horses but in big trucks. The gang would pull up to a house and empty its contents into the truck.

"How do they get in?" I asked one volunteer.

"Oh, it's easy," he replied. "They knock the door down."

No wonder Joe was frustrated and miserable. He wanted a real adventure, not a third-world version of his life in New York City. Every time I saw him, he talked about how he needed to get out of Freetown and have a real African experience. "Look at me," he would say, "I even eat hamburgers for dinner."

Meanwhile, Adrienne and I were having about as much of an adventure as we could handle. Living in Africa turned out to be harder than we had anticipated. After training, the Peace Corps assigned us to Bumpe, a village of about three thousand, set along the main road, about a hundred miles up-country from Freetown.

The night we arrived, the village chief, Senesee Fogbawa, came to our house to greet us. He wore a Shriner-shaped hat, a long ceremonial robe down to his ankles, and Adidas gym shoes. I thought the scrawny chicken he held under his arm was a pet. Then he smiled a big, gold-toothed smile and handed the chicken to me. It was a welcoming present.

I was used to chicken coming fried on a plate. Panicked, I thought "chicken coop." How do I make a chicken coop? Where do I get chicken feed? "Please," I said, handing the chicken back to him, "can you keep him for us until we're ready?" I didn't know that in Sierra Leone chickens wander all over and eat whatever they can find. With a puzzled look, Chief Fogbawa took the chicken back. I never saw it alive again. Two days later as I was walking by the chief's house, he gave me that same gold-toothed smile and waved a drumstick at me.

We got other presents of food, too. Sometimes a neighbor would bring us a breakfast of oily fish, rice, and hot peppers, then wait around to see how we liked it.

One night the children set up lanterns and pots of water. When dusk fell, the air was filled with a flying insect we hadn't seen before. The larvae must have just hatched. They looked something like wasps. The insects flew into the lanterns, and the children knocked them into the water, singing the whole time. We thought it was charming. Then they fried the insects and ate them. Of course, we received a large gift of that special delicacy.

Actually, we should have eaten them with relish, just for revenge. Once we began living in Bumpe, we understood the chocolate chip incident at the airport. Bugs were everywhere. You had to get used to them or you'd go mad. For instance, ants constantly roamed our walls, aimlessly looking for food and trying to avoid the spiders that roosted up by the roof. Every now and then our kerosene refrigerator would run out of fuel. We could always tell because the ants would suddenly line up and march straight toward the fridge. Once we got the refrigerator restarted we had to deal with the ant-laden food. We couldn't just throw it all out; our closest grocery store was fifteen miles away. So we had to learn to manage.

One day ants got into the bag of sugar Adrienne had been

planning to use in a cake. A few months earlier she would have been horrified, but now an experienced Adrienne decided on a chocolate cake for camouflage. She poured the sugar and ant mixture into her mixing bowl and began to crush the ants against the sides with her spoon. More were baked to death when the cake was placed in the oven. Finally, she put the cake in the refrigerator, freezing the rest. The cake was wonderful. The ants looked like poppy seeds, as long as you didn't get a piece with little legs dangling in the air.

The bugs I could get used to; the snakes I couldn't. They had a snake in Sierra Leone called a green mamba that could kill you in thirty seconds. In its wisdom the Peace Corps had placed our nearest snake kit fifteen miles away.

When I asked Chief Fogbawa what the townspeople did about snakes, he told me not to worry—they had a snakeman whose job it was to kill them. My first sight of Abu was of a man dancing down the street in the pouring rain, mysteriously swinging an eight-foot pole from side to side. The man came to a stop, raised the pole high over one shoulder, and froze in that position. Then he smashed the pole against the ground. He smiled, bent down, and picked up a ten-foot snake that had been heading in my direction.

One night a spitting cobra came to our house. It probably was after our cat. Later I found out that spitting cobras spit in your eyes to blind you, then kill you at their leisure. All I knew that night was that a long snake had slithered through our front door. Adrienne and I leaped onto our kitchen table, screaming "kali, kali!" We hoped we were using the right tone and that our neighbors weren't wondering why we were so excited about a stick.

When Abu arrived at our house, we pointed at the bedroom where the snake had disappeared. Abu entered, put his pole down on the bed, and began to lift up boots and open drawers. I thought he was a dead man. Even I knew that a cornered snake would something in the corner. A few seconds later, he emerged carrying the dead snake. We were told later that it was a baby, only five feet long.

I asked my headmaster why the snake hadn't attacked Abu. "Oh," he replied, with a casual shake of his head, "he has snake magic." When he saw the skepticism on my face, he added, "He chews a special concoction of herbs and then rubs it on his body. It makes the snake sleepy."

Yes, Bumpe certainly wasn't Chicago. We didn't ask what the weather was before we went swimming; we asked if the water was low enough so that the crocodiles wouldn't be in the river. We didn't just go to the outhouse; we carried insect spray, a swatter, and a stick because we never knew what we would have to fight off once we got there. We didn't go to the corner butcher store to get neatly cut steaks; we stood in an open air market where a man hacked at a piece of bloody meat that was hanging from a hook and covered with flies. It was enough to turn us into non-swimming, constipated vegetarians.

There was no telling what odd thing was going to happen on any given day. Take the time our house collapsed. The worst houses in the village were small mud huts with thatched roofs and dirt floors. Most houses, however, had thick whitewashed walls, made up of mud and sticks, a tin roof, and a cement floor. Our five-room house was built like that.

One night as we lay under our mosquito netting, we heard a cracking sound.

"What's that?" Adrienne asked.

I joked that it sounded as if our house were falling apart.

We went back to sleep but a few minutes later we heard a tremendous crash. Adrienne leaped out of bed and ran toward the kitchen. "My God, Syd," she yelled, "I can see the sky." It seemed our kitchen walls had caved out. I joined her and we stood there as if we were on stage. Scene: Peace Corps volunteers in kitchen at night.

A number of our neighbors in nightclothes stood outside staring at us as if they were watching a late-night movie. "Boo-ah," one said, the Mende word for hello.

What else was there to say? "Boo-ah," we replied.

At times I couldn't take it. "Third world" didn't seem like the right appellation. Sierra Leone seemed like the eighth world. I went for a walk in the rice fields the day we landed a man on the moon. A boy perched on a straw platform, just staring out into space. When some birds approached, the boy rose, grabbed a mud ball from a pile at his side, put it in a sling, and whipped the mud ball at the birds. When they flew away, the boy squatted back down. He was a living scarecrow, a page out of prehistory. Some days I wanted just to close my shutters, lock the door, read *Newsweek*, listen to the Beatles, and eat Skippy peanut butter out of the jar.

But Joe was undaunted in his search for adventure, even when I told him about the spitting cobra or our house collapsing. He stared sadly, like a man who sees his last chance disappearing. "I've got to get up-country," he'd whisper.

And now, at last, Joe was going to get his chance. I jumped into the Land Rover and we roared off. "Are you going to tell me where we're headed?" I asked after awhile.

Joe flashed his sly smile. "Syd," he said, "this is it. They're opening up a high school way off in the bush. It's further up-country than any other school has ever been. The principal called to invite me to a huge celebration—maybe all night, he said—and I'm the guest of honor because I head the Peace Corps teaching program in country. Look, I'm wearing my best tie-dye shirt and I've got all the gear I need." He reached behind him and pulled into the front seat a backpack that contained a camera and tape recorder. "I'm going to capture the whole thing." He beeped his horn again and again and began to dance in his seat.

And so we rolled down the road. Joe was aching to experience the heart and soul of this slumbering giant of a continent, ready to capture the beat and rhythm of its people on Kodak and Memorex. And I was his Sancho Panza.

We sped down the highway. After a few hours Joe stopped at a roadside cafe and ordered some rice, chicken, and peppers.

"How hot you want?" asked the proprietor.

"As hot as you eat it," said Joe. He turned toward me. "You want some?" I passed because I knew how hot it would be. Some food presents had been impossible to eat.

Sweat poured off Joe as he ate. He managed to maintain a smile the whole time even though his mouth must have been on fire. A small crowd had gathered around us to see what would happen to him. "Great," he managed to gasp out after he downed his third soft drink. The crowd smiled and one woman even clapped as we left.

Soon Joe left the main road. He cut off on a dirt road. The road got smaller and smaller until it was down to a couple of ruts, but on we flew. We were way up-country. The wilder it got, the happier Joe got. He excitedly pointed out trees and monkeys, even insects on the windshield. I felt as if I were with Marlin Perkins on *Wild Kingdom.* "This is it," Joe yelled as he beat me on the shoulder. "This is the real Africa. I'm finally going to experience it!"

We roared around a turn, the bush suddenly parted, and the village opened in front of us. Joe slammed on his brakes, and we skidded to a halt. He blinked his eyes. He blinked them again. He rubbed them as if he wanted to make sure that he wasn't seeing a mirage. He looked at me as if to make sure I was there and this wasn't a dream. Then he looked at the village again.

You see, we had forgotten the truth of the saying that the grass is always greener in the other guy's yard. All the Peace Corps volunteers were trying to be African. We wore Mende tie-dyed clothes and tried to eat Mende food, hot enough to burn our tongues off. Well, the Mende were no different. They wanted to wear ready-made clothes and drink Coke. So there before us stood a whole village of people looking as if they had bought their clothes from the Sears catalogue.

We pulled slowly into town, passing through the swirling mass of American-looking Mende people. Joe was crestfallen. He actually appeared to shrink in his seat. A smiling teacher from the new school directed us toward the center of town. "We have a surprise for you," he said. And they did: a brass band.

Their instruments glowed in the setting sun. Their black and yellow nylon uniforms, probably donated by an American high school, glistened. They must have been waiting for Joe, the guest of honor, because as soon as we got out of the Land Rover, the conductor raised his baton, the band began to play, and the villagers started to sing:

The dance of Mexico will help you to fall in love.
The dance of Mexico will help you to fall in love.
Olé, ola, olita, take the arm of your sweet Señorita
Olé, ola, olita, you're doing a Mexican dance.

When the song ended, the principal who had invited Joe came over and said, "I bet you weren't expecting a brass band. I kept it a secret!"

"No," Joe replied weakly. "I wasn't."

Joe wore a sickly smile the whole time we ate and the band played a medley of folk songs from around the world, including "Swanee River." As soon as he could, Joe began a series of gracious good-byes. As we were getting into the Land Rover, the principal rushed up to Joe and pleaded, "Stay, please stay. Later on they are going to play Sousa marches."

The ride back to Bumpe was long and quiet. It was late at night when we got there and everything was closed except Mariama's bar. A few farmers were squatting out in front, drinking palm wine. "C'mon, Joe," I said, "I'll buy you a jug."

"Naw, Syd," he replied, "you better make mine a Coke."

The Irregulars

The day before school opened, the principal told me that thanks to a scheduling snafu I would start the year teaching only four classes instead of the usual five. When he assured me that they would have the fifth class ready for me in a few weeks, I wanted to tell him to take his time. This was my first job after returning from the Peace Corps, and easing my way back into the working world gradually sounded ideal. If I had known how they were going to create the new class, I might have contacted the Peace Corps and re-upped.

Three weeks later the principal sent a notice to all sophomore teachers:

> We need to create another section of 2 English Regular. Send the names of three students for this new class to your department chairman by the end of the week. Please make them representative of the total make-up of the student population.

I looked out the window expecting to see snow. After all, what the principal had just done was to turn himself into the Santa Claus of the sophomore teachers. For no matter how often they tell you in teacher training that you have to love and treat all the little darlings equally, every teacher knows that you just want to strangle some kids. And it's about three weeks into the school year when the thought begins to sink in that you are going to have to see those kids every day for the next nine months. To the sophomore teachers, the principal's note must have read like a governor's death-row reprieve.

Castro could have taken lessons from these teachers; they emptied their classrooms of all their misfits and undesirables. I didn't inherit any really bad discipline problems, but I did get strange kids, ones whose wires weren't connected exactly right. The gamut ranged from weird to weirder. The class might have been officially listed as "regular"—between remedial and honors—but after the very first morning, I dubbed the group the irregulars.

Sullen and upset about having to change into a new class, they trudged into my room. A black girl pushed her way through the crowd of the condemned and charged up to me. "My mother is calling and if this is some dumb class, she's getting me out."

"It's not a dumb class," I protested. "It's a regular—"

"Just don't expect me to do any work today," she continued haughtily. "I'm not doing any work for a class I'm getting out of." With that, she headed to a seat, muttering all the way.

"Dumb class," said a white boy in a T-shirt who was seated right in front of me. "I ain't no dummy."

"You ain't?" asked a black boy seated next to him.

"Well, maybe I am," answered the white boy, and the two high-fived each other and laughed.

By the time the bell rang, they had all managed to find a seat except for one boy who stood patiently about five feet away from me. He was dressed neatly in a short-sleeved checked shirt and blue slacks, and he held a Monopoly game under one arm.

I motioned toward a seat, but he just stood there, pleasantly smiling at me. "Is there some problem?" I asked.

"Can we play Monopoly today?" he replied, pulling the game out from under his arm.

"What's your name?"

"Donald."

"Well, Donald, this is school." I motioned around the room in case he hadn't noticed. "This is a sophomore English class. We won't be playing Monopoly in here. Now please grab a seat so we can begin."

I turned to the class, but Donald just stood there.

"Donald," I said, "a seat."

"Can we play tomorrow?" he asked. His request was so sincere that no one laughed.

"No, Donald," I said gently. "We won't play tomorrow. We won't play the next day. We're just not going to play Monopoly in here. Now please take a seat."

Donald didn't seem unduly upset as he headed toward the back of the room. I found out why the next day when he arrived carrying Clue. Donald was indefatigable. Wednesday he spilled dominoes on my desk. Thursday he opened a checkers board in front of me and beamed as if he were presenting a new baby. Friday, he suggested chess. On Monday, Donald started all over again, but this time he presented the games in a different order. It was as if he were trying to conjure up the right combination of game and day, a combination I would agree to, a combination that would shake dice out of the sky so the games could finally begin.

When Donald found his seat, I began my first-day pep talk. That's when I noticed an enormous black girl in the back row. She was so large I couldn't imagine how she had wedged herself into the desk. But there she sat, admiring herself in the mirror of a tiny pink compact case.

"Excuse me," I said, "but class has started."

She shrugged and kept studying herself. "I'm listening."

"What's your name?"

"Sheila."

"Well, Sheila, you need to put away the make-up. Now!"

"Oh no," said another girl in the back. "Here it comes."

Sheila gave me a shocked look, bit her lip, and grabbed her desk. She looked as if she were holding her breath. Then both she and the desk began to quiver and shake, and Sheila began to cry. Huge, racking sobs rose from the center of her being.

"Sheila," I shouted, "why are you crying? What's the matter?"

Sheila just sobbed louder.

"Excuse me, teacher," said a small black girl from the back of the room. "I'm Sheila's cousin, Erika. She won't stop unless you apologize for yelling at her."

"Apologize?" I replied. "She was the one with the make-up case."

Sheila's cousin just shrugged. "Yeah, but you'll have to apologize anyway. She's just like that."

A number of kids shook their heads in agreement. Everyone seemed to know about Sheila. They waited patiently for my apology.

"Sheila," I said, "I apologize for yelling at you." But Sheila wouldn't even look at me. She just stared at her desk and, through sobs, shook her head no.

"Teacher," said her cousin, "you need to get down and look her in the face." Erika turned her head sideways to illustrate how it should be done. Several students joined her.

I had to get down on one knee to catch her eye. "Sheila," I said gently, "I'm sorry for yelling, but you need to put your make-up away. OK?"

Sheila looked at me to see if I really meant my apology.

I shook my head yes.

Slowly her sobs subsided. She pulled a king-size Kleenex box out of her purse, dabbed her eyes, and blew her nose. Then she put her Kleenex box and her make-up case away and proffered a small smile.

"See," said her cousin, my mentor.

By the end of the week, I began to get a feel for all their peculiarities. Her cousin was right; Sheila cried every time I spoke harshly to her. Laurie sucked her thumb. Lee would fall asleep every day because he was exhausted from work and basketball practice. I had to make him walk up and down in the back of the room so he would stay awake. He looked as if he were on guard duty. Mary was so shy she didn't say anything even when I called on her. The first time I heard her voice was December. It took her twenty minutes to get up the courage to tell me I had forgotten to give her a handout. Susie must have been born bored. She'd chomp on her gum, play with her teased hair, and look miserable no matter what we did.

Andre and Jeff posed the only potential discipline problem. Best friends, the boys seemed different in every way. Jeff was short, stocky, and white. Andre was tall, slim, and black. Jeff acted as if he were running for class clown, Andre as if he were majoring in coolness. But they were both starting guards on the football team and inseparable buddies. Jeff and Andre arrived together, sat together, and left together. They also punched each other every chance they got. As soon as I'd turn around to write something on the board, I'd hear a punch land and one of them would snigger. When I turned back, they'd be sitting there like cherubs, only one or the other would be rubbing his shoulder.

Once I managed to get that behavior under control, Jeff created a new problem. He decided that he wasn't going to get up from his desk throughout the entire class. If he had to get a pencil sharpened, if he had to get a book, if I called on him to write something on the blackboard, he would just wrap his legs around the chair legs and back up to wherever he was going. "Out of my way," he would shout. "Toot, toot, out of my way."

One day after writing on the board, I turned around to find that Jeff and his desk were gone. "Where's Jeff?" I asked.

"He's out in the hall," said Andre. "He wanted to see how much speed he could get up on a straightaway."

I rushed to the door. Sure enough, there was Jeff hunched over and jerking from side to side as he pushed his chair quickly down the hall. When he saw me, he waved merrily.

"Get back in here," I shouted.

Jeff gave me a thumbs-up sign, made a U-turn around a very confused teacher, and chugged back to class.

The strange thing about the irregulars was how well they seemed to accept each other's oddness. If you had observed my class, you would have thought I was running a carnival sideshow. "See Sheila the Cryer, Donald the Gamesman, Jeff and his Dynamo Chair." But nobody made fun of Laurie when she sucked her thumb. Everyone waited for Sheila to get over her fits of crying. No one imitated Jeff and Andre when they punched each other. No one chimed in when bored Susie complained. They all tried to help Lee stay awake. And I even overheard one student tell Donald that he would play checkers with him at lunch. To the participants, the sideshow is just life. The kids accepted each other no matter how strangely they acted because that's just the way they were.

I soon came to appreciate them, too. But teaching them was another matter. In November we started *Macbeth.* I knew the language would be hard for them, so every day in class I played a videotape of the portion they had read the night before. I encouraged them to ask about anything, and I repeatedly assured them that no question was dumb.

Late in the play Ross comes to Macduff to tell him that Macbeth has murdered his wife and children. The news, of course, is overwhelming for Macduff. On the BBC version the kids were watching, Macduff grits his teeth and grabs Ross's shoulders to keep from falling. As if he can't fathom the news, Macduff keeps repeating the message:

...All my pretty ones?
Did you say all? O hell-kite! All?
What, all my pretty chickens and their dam
At one fell swoop?

After the scene ended, Andre wore a puzzled look on his face. He raised his hand and haltingly asked, "Did Macbeth really kill his chickens, too?" No one laughed. They just sat there, waiting expectantly for my answer. I had never been asked that question before. It occurred to me that I might have sent a generation of students out into the world believing that Macbeth was a chicken killer.

To avoid wholesale failure, I gave them a chance to do extra credit. I knew that this class needed a wide range of possibilities, so I just asked them to do an essay or an art project that related to the material we had studied that year.

As soon as I said that, Jeff's hand shot into the air. "Mr. Lieberman, what did we study this year?"

Predictably, the extra credit projects were a dismal failure. Rachel, a girl from Haiti, brought in an essay which she claimed described her life back home. It contained a lyrical description of snow falling gently on green fields dotted with cows and sheep.

Nassar, a boy from Egypt, handed me a painting of what looked like Rachel's landscape. He didn't claim it was his home, but he did claim to have painted it. When I pointed out the machine-made fake brush strokes carved into the cardboard canvas and the spot where the price tag had been peeled off, Nassar exited in a huff.

Jeff brought in a plastic model of a space ship.

"Jeff," I said, "we didn't read any science fiction this year."

"We didn't?" he replied.

He swore he had just constructed the ship for extra credit, but it needed a dusting.

Donald tried to convince me to allow him to organize a dominoes tournament and Susie complained every day that she wasn't going to do extra credit because it was too boring.

Victor was another student who didn't attempt extra credit. I don't think he understood the concept. He certainly didn't understand much English. His essays were complete gibberish. I swear he wrote in Chinese, his native language, and had one of his family members translate his writing verbatim. But God bless him, he turned in all his assignments, and he showed up every day beaming at me as if I were a symbol of his new country. One day I asked him what he thought he deserved as a grade. Without a moment of indecision, he smiled and said, "C+."

The saddest extra credit project was Gerald's. A slow, teddy-bear blob of a kid, Gerald was as sweet as he was thick. Everything went wrong for him. Gerald would write down the wrong pages for a homework assignment. He'd drop his work into a puddle on the way to school. His dog ate his copy of *The Old Man and the Sea.*

Gerald's hobby was making models out of toothpicks. He asked me if he could make a model of Odysseus's boat, and even though we hadn't studied *The Odyssey,* I agreed.

The day the assignment was due, Gerald shuffled in, holding a shoe box away from his body as if he didn't want anything to do with it.

"What's the problem?" I asked.

He looked at me shamefaced, rocked from foot to foot, and pulled the model out. It consisted of half a boat glued to a cardboard base that he had painted blue. The back half was just a mass of toothpicks scattered about.

"Look's like your ship was torpedoed," I said. "What happened?"

"This morning at breakfast," he mumbled, looking ready to cry. "I sat on it."

Late in the semester, Walter entered the class. He was a huge black guy about 6'4" and 250 pounds. Without a word, he handed me a sealed envelope. I ripped it open and read a one-line message from the principal. "We moved Walter to your class because we think he needs a man." Terrific, I thought. That's just what I need, just what this class needs—me becoming a father figure for Goliath. But I straightened up my 5'6 1/2" frame, tugged at my belt, and invited him to take a seat. Walter sat as far away from me as he could get. Then he slowly folded his arms, leaned back, and began to scowl. He had the presence of a sullen mountain.

I let Walter sit like that way for a week. I knew that he would need time to adjust to the strange atmosphere of the class. Every day Walter would take a seat in the back and stare balefully at me, daring me to challenge him to move a muscle.

Walter's presence hushed the whole class. Donald didn't even ask him if he wanted to play a game, and Jeff went about his work without the usual horsing around.

After a week, I decided to call on Walter. Who knows, I thought, maybe he just feels left out. So during a discussion of *The Glass Menagerie*, I tossed out a softball question, pointed at Walter, and casually said, "Why don't you try it?"

Walter leaped to his feet, clinched his hands into fists and shouted, "Don't you point at me, man. Don't you point at me."

Usually when a student calls me man, I remind him that my name is *Lieber*man. But this didn't seem like the right time for the lesson. Walter stood there, huffing and puffing and ready to charge. Like a bullfighter, I waved an imaginary cape toward the door and whispered, "Walter, why don't you leave? Just leave." Walter crashed past me without a word.

"Don't worry," said Sheila, "he's like that in all his classes. I'm surprised he even comes." Several students nodded in agreement.

"Wow!" said Susie. For a second, something had gotten her

attention. Then she must have remembered that she was bored, and returned to staring out the window and chomping away on her gum.

I didn't report the incident. Walter had been in a number of fights, and I had been told that he would be expelled if he got into any trouble.

Two days later he returned. If he was surprised that I hadn't turned him in, he didn't show it. He just took his seat in the back of the room and tracked me with his usual hostile stare.

The kids stayed out of his way. They didn't look at him or talk to him. That is, everyone except Donald. Donald decided to welcome Walter back. "Want to play checkers?" he asked.

"What?" Walter roared, spinning toward him.

Donald looked scared but his love of games made him press on. "Checkers," he said, opening the board as if that would make Walter understand.

Walter stared at the board for a few seconds before Donald's request finally registered. For a moment he relaxed. "No man ... No," Walter said.

"That's OK," said Donald, "I'll ask you again tomorrow."

Walter gave him a fraction of a smile. Then he tightened again and turned toward me with the familiar sullen expression frozen on his face.

The exchange took only a few moments, but it gave me an epiphany about Walter. Walter wasn't any different than the other kids. He was just another irregular. Walter was the sideshow's strung-out gun hand who sees a challenge in every look, a battle with the approach of every stranger.

He wasn't playing an easy role. Because he was a big black male, I'm sure he had been confronted a lot in his short life. How many of those confrontations does it take to turn someone into a coiled spring?

At the end of class, I asked Walter to stay for a second. He loomed up at my side, towering over me, ready for a fight. I'm sure he expected me to read him out or at least talk about his conduct. Instead, I said, "Walter, everybody blows up sometimes. You look like the kind of guy who needs to explode a little more than some others." Walter looked completely puzzled, but I plowed on.

"We don't have to have a scene every time you need to explode. If you feel like you're going to blow, just give me a little nod. I'll find a reason to send you out of class. I'll send you on an errand or something. OK?" Walter didn't answer. He seemed unsure about whether I had finished. Then, without saying a word, he left.

The normal cold war between us continued. Then on Friday, in the middle of an explanation of when you use a comma before a coordinating conjunction, I noticed Walter imperceptibly shaking his head up and down. The movement was so slight, I wasn't sure I was actually seeing it. I continued talking and looked at Walter with a quizzical look in my eyes. In response, Walter shook his head a little more.

"Oh," I said, feigning surprise, "I just remembered that I have a note to take down to the office." Before I could ask for a volunteer, every hand shot up but Walter's. "How about you, Walter?" I asked. The class sat there dumbfounded as Walter stood at the edge of my desk, waiting for a hall pass.

Walter had to leave about a half dozen times that year. I never knew where he went. I never asked and Walter never told. But he didn't get into any trouble and he made it through the year.

I'd like to say that Walter became the leader of the class; that Sheila learned not to cry; that Susie became jovial; that Victor learned English; that Andre and Jeff became model students; and that Donald stopped bringing a game to class every day. Of course, they didn't. They ended pretty much the way they began, a ragtag, bedraggled, befuddled, and befuddling group of misfits.

But I think they learned a lesson that year, or maybe they knew the lesson all along and taught it to me: everyone is somebody's baby. As Jim Post, a folk singer, says in one of his songs, everyone is somebody's "jump for joy." As odd as they were, they treated each other and me with respect. Maybe because of their oddness, they knew what their odd peers needed—to be loved and cared for and somehow cherished for themselves.

By the way, I finally did allow Donald to have a games tournament on the last day of class. "Thank you, Mr. Lieberman," he said, shaking my hand. "Thank you." Everyone played except Walter.

I saw Walter once that summer. He was riding a bicycle in front of the school. When he saw me, he took his hands off the handlebars and, of all things, smiled. "How you doing, old man?" he yelled as he rode by. "How you doing?"

"Fine," I called after him. I wanted to ask him how he was doing but he was already past me, waving back with one hand over his head. I stood for a minute watching him breeze off, no-handed, into the distance.

The Italian T-Shirt

The kids were one and three at the time. My wife was going grocery shopping and I figured to get a little writing done while I baby-sat the kids. When I told Adrienne my plans, she rolled her eyes as if to say, "What a virgin." She smirked as she went out the door, looking as if she'd been released from jail.

But I was confident. As soon as Adrienne left, I got the kids started on projects, my three-year-old daughter painting at the kitchen table, my one-year-old son banging around on one of those Playskool work benches.

I felt rather proud of myself as I tiptoed out of the kitchen, but before I even sat down at the typewriter, Sarah's blood-curdling screams shattered the peace. I rushed back to the kitchen to find Zach beating his sister over the head with a toy hammer. "Zach," I yelled. He turned, and to show me he wasn't picking favorites, with a big smile, he began to beat himself over the head, too. I didn't know whether I should stop him. He seemed so happy.

"Look, Daddy," said Sarah, suddenly recovered. With one hand she was proudly sand painting with some sugar she had spilled all over the kitchen floor, and with the other she was squeezing margarine into Henry Moore-type sculptures.

As soon as I got her mess cleaned up and both of them staring at the television, I headed back toward the typewriter.

But then the phone began ringing. A car agency wanted to fix me up, an insurance company wanted to sign me up, a heavy breather wanted to pick me up.

The morning continued apace. Zach pulled a five-hundred-piece puzzle off the shelf and happily mixed it up with another five-hundred-piece puzzle. Sarah spilled a quart of milk in the refrigerator. I tried to bake chocolate chip cookies and burned them. I reached the nadir of the morning when I went to take the garbage out and the bag broke. It was an existential moment, standing there and watching dirty Pampers blow all over my backyard. I felt like the man in the Glad Bag ads.

It didn't take much from Adrienne to set me off. She stood in the doorway and sized up the scene, looking a little bit like a Red Cross volunteer surveying a disaster area. As if I had been torturing them, the kids ran to her and each clutched a leg. "I can't believe all this happened while I was shopping," she said incredulously. The kids stared at me as if they couldn't believe it either. "What were you doing? Weren't you even watching them?"

"Watching them? Watching them!" I grabbed my coat and started out the door. "They can drive you crazy! I'm getting out of here."

"Sure," she yelled after me, "you can't even handle them for a couple of hours. Try having them for a whole day." In my hurry I knocked one of the grocery bags down the stairs. Adrienne's silent stare and a trail of eggs followed me down the street.

But my troubles didn't end there. A neighbor blocked my path and waved a finger in my face. "Park in front of your own house," he shouted. "Be neighborly!" Just then a little cocker spaniel jumped up to bite me. "Never seen him do that before," said his owner.

I was down in the dumps: depressed, upset, angry. I walked for a long time, just staring at the ground. Suddenly, an inner voice told me to look up. When I did, I saw my salvation right there in front of me. For there in the center of a men's store window, below an "On Sale" sign, on a beige headless dummy, sat an Italian T-shirt.

That shirt took me back to my teen years in Albany Park on Chicago's Northwest side. In those days Albany Park was predominantly a Jewish neighborhood, but it also contained a sizable Italian population. The Italian guys fascinated me. They hung out in Ma's, their own smoke-filled store across the street from the high school. They wore black leather jackets and tank tops with thin spaghetti straps. We called those tank tops Italian T-shirts because we Jewish guys wore the regular kind of T-shirts with short sleeves. Something about those Italian T-shirts—the way they showed off shoulders and biceps—made them seem so cool.

And it was in one those Italian T-shirts that I could see Jimmy again, the original out of which they would make the parodies, like Fonzie.

Picture this. It was the first week of a new school year. I was sitting in a last period history class. Up in front of me, the teacher droned on about dates and facts. Every now and then, as if to keep us awake, he cleared his throat in the middle of a sentence.

He was a thin man with an Adam's apple that bobbed up and down when he talked, and a dirty blond crew cut that was waxed straight up, making him look like an odd bird. Mr. Vernon's plumage included a blue suit; an Indian bead belt; and brown Keds, the old kind with the canvas tops and large crepe soles. His different parts looked as if they were going to different parties.

Green corrugated cardboard paper covered the walls with last year's dusty displays. Six cream-colored globes hung from the ceiling, pretending to be lighting the room. In the winter I could take it. When the weather was frozen, I could flip paper clips into the desk's inkwell. I could while away the minutes by reading the messages other prisoners of war had carved in the desk.

But this was the first week of school. Summer had been teasing us by hanging around. The breezes wafted in, as enticing as a siren's call. Even worse, when I looked out the window, there was Jimmy, cutting school the very first week.

He rested against his '55 Chevy. You know the kind: oversized dice hanging from the rear view mirror, the back end jacked up, statues of football players with swiveling heads posted in the back window. Jimmy calmly leaned there, his arms folded in front of him, surveying the building to see if it was a Goliath worthy of his battle.

Jimmy resembled a young Marlon Brando. His hair curled down over his forehead in a careful wave, and smoke curled up from the cigarette dangling in the corner of his lip. The large gold cross he wore was easy to see because all he had on was blue jeans and a skin-tight white Italian T-shirt. Jimmy looked so cool and tough that the American Revolution and Mr. Vernon, its blue bird spokesman, didn't have a chance for my attention.

But it wasn't just what Jimmy wore. He was cool and tough. Once, coming back from a baseball game, a guy said, "Hey, Jimmy, I'll bet you ten bucks you won't jump off the next bridge." Jimmy smiled and when we got there, he jumped right off. He landed in the sewage canal and broke his leg, but he won the bet.

Another time Jimmy and I were walking through a park coming home from a baseball game when a guy staring at Jimmy yelled, "Hey, look at the greasy wop." The guy was in his twenties, playing first base for a man's team. They wore bright red jerseys advertising a neighborhood bar. When he yelled, his buddies began to smirk.

Jimmy was a little guy—about 5' 5"—and he walked up to the big guy without saying a word. The big guy put his hands on his hips and leaned over as if to say, "So, Pipsqueak, what are you going to do about it?" His friends began laughing. Jimmy tilted his head and looked at the guy as if he was sizing him up. Then without warning, Jimmy swung the spikes he was carrying and whapped the guy in the face. Blood spurted out. The big guy fell to the ground; Jimmy was all over him. This was violence—real violence.

What did I know about violence? I came close to it only once when the club I belonged to, the Condors, almost got into a gang fight. Usually, we were involved in wholesome activities. We held mixers with girls' clubs, which at best meant necking, and at least chips and Cokes. We played in sports leagues arranged by the Albany Park Jewish Community Center against teams called the Anacondas and the Torpedoes. Our cool orange and blue reversible jackets had Condors written in orange on one side and a large blue "C" on the other.

Then we heard that another club was starting up at a different high school, and they were going to call themselves the Condors. We decided that rather than let this happen we would fight. So there we were in a local park late one night, ready for our first gang fight: twenty middle-class, scared-to-death Jewish guys holding baseball bats, waiting for twenty other middle-class, scared-to-death Jewish guys to show up with their baseball bats.

To everyone's relief, even though we didn't admit it, we never got a chance to fight. The two club presidents and an adult leader resolved the crisis at the local Jewish community center.

But Jimmy was familiar with violence. Even though he hung out with us—mostly because he liked sports—he generally ran with a rough crowd. The tales Jimmy told of his other world seemed as fantastic to us as the adventures of Odysseus. His friend Stork was gunned down and killed in an attempted robbery his senior year. Another friend, who called himself Dirt, knocked a policeman down and stole his gun so he could use it in holdups. Jimmy knew about marijuana before we had even heard the word. And he was suspended for walking down the hallway with his arm around Roberta, his girl. When the principal told Jimmy he couldn't do that, Jimmy's reply got him thrown out of school.

Is it any wonder that the T-shirt in the window of the store looked so cool and tough to me? How many chances do I get to be cool and tough? Have you ever seen fashion ads featuring English teachers? Have you seen any movies starring teachers handing out detentions? What could I be: Kojak of the washrooms? Sonny Crockett of the hallways?

And unless you're Michael Jordan, it's hard to look cool and tough when you're bald. I'd been bald for a long time. My college graduation picture shows me staring off into the I'll-conquer-the-world void under a reasonably full head of hair. A photo taken just six years later shows me wearing a dopey grin beneath a shiny pate.

In the late sixties and early seventies, everyone I knew wore his hair long. Many had hair down to their shoulders. God knows, I tried, but all I could manage was two curly clumps on the sides. One day my niece looked quizzically at me and said, "You look like Bozo the clown." Around that same time I had a student who said I reminded her of a koala bear. The whole class stopped writing, looked up, and agreed, "Yahhhh!" A koala bear! Now who wants to grow up and be a cuddly, cute koala bear? I had always wanted to be a black bear or a grizzly bear.

Yet every time I get a chance to be cool or tough, I blow it. The night I told Adrienne I loved her, we stood on a bridge overlooking the Charles River in Boston. The evening should have been really romantic, but it was ear-aching-and-nose-nipping freezing outside, especially on a bridge exposed to the wind. We were afraid to kiss; we thought our lips might stick together.

We decided to warm up in the Back Bay, where we found a coffee shop in a small hotel. It looked like a set from a movie: romantic little tables for two, smoky gold mirrors, and a huge chandelier. The place was empty when we entered. Who, except for a couple of crazed lovers, would be out on a night like that? We ordered coffee and doughnuts.

The waiter served us, and disappeared into the back. Romantic music suddenly began to waft through the tiny establishment. The perfect moment had coalesced around us. I thought of the movie *The Hustler* staring Paul Newman. In that film his girl, Piper Laurie, orders a meal, and when the waiter turns to Paul, he never looks away from Piper. He just holds up two fingers near the side of his head and says, "Two."

It seemed so cool to me. I knew what I wanted to do. I figured I'd stare right into Adrienne's eyes, grab her hand, and say, "I love you" at the same time. I gave her my best look, reached out, leaned back, and just kept going. As I was falling, I remember wondering what was smeared all over my fingers. I had grabbed her jelly doughnut instead of her hand. "I looooove you … BOOOM!"

When the saleswoman started to put the T-shirt into the bag, I said, "Wait a minute. I'll wear it." And right there in the store, I took off my shirt and put on my first Italian T-shirt. You won't believe this, but tattoos started to bulge out on my arms. No longer was I a little, bald, Jewish koala bear. I had become a swarthy Italian, capable of love or danger at the drop of a hat. You think Belker invented the snarl on *Hill Street Blues*? When a man gave me a funny look, I growled at him; he darted behind the underwear.

I walked outside, scratched my chest hair, and sniffed my armpits. I felt like Brando in *A Streetcar Named Desire.* Men got out of my way. Women looked at me suggestively. Dogs tucked their tails between their legs and ran.

I sauntered home like John Travolta at the start of *Saturday Night Fever.* When I got to my house, I jumped into my car—my Plymouth Volare station wagon—and drove it right in front of my neighbor's home. I parked the car, got out, folded my arms, and leaned against it. I wished I had a cigarette and a gold cross, but I looked so cool and tough, I didn't even need them. My neighbor took one look and pulled his shade straight down. I felt like Bogie at the end of *Casablanca.*

When I entered my house, I went straight for the second-story bedroom window. I sat in it, singing a fake aria to the whole neighborhood. Kids laughed and waved. A cop drove by, probably called by my neighborly neighbor, but all he did was smile and give me a thumbs-up signal.

Adrienne came home just as I was finishing. I leaned out the window and sang the last few fake Italian lines to her. The moment was worthy of *The Godfather.* She looked up and shook her head in disbelief. When she entered the house, she yelled, "You must be nuts. I could hear you a block away. I took the kids to my sister's. They were driving me crazy, too." She started to say something else, but she never got a chance. Because thinking Paul Newman, Marlon Brando, John Travolta, and Humphrey Bogart, but especially Jimmy, I sucked in my gut, went downstairs, picked her up, and carried her off. If my old principal had seen what came next, he'd have thrown us both out of school.

The Day the Nazis Came

When the Nazis declared that they were going to speak at a park not more than a mile from my house, I didn't pay much attention. Two years earlier, in 1978, they had announced a march in Skokie, a suburb with a large population of concentration camp survivors. That announcement had turned out to be nothing but a publicity stunt. But as the date of the speech approached and it began to look as if this event would actually take place, I grew increasingly upset.

For most of my life being a Jew hadn't been a big issue. Growing up in a Jewish neighborhood made being Jewish easy. We took it for granted that you could find a deli or a Jewish bakery on just about every block, that synagogues were liberally sprinkled throughout the area, that the public schools would empty out on Jewish holidays. We got along with the Christians in the neighborhood, so we didn't have to struggle to be Jewish.

The same was true at Harvard. Though finals clubs shunned Jewish members, I had many Jewish classmates.

When my wife and I decided to buy a house, we settled in Evanston, a liberal community on the North Shore that has a large population of both Jews and Blacks. So I had lived my life in comfortable settings. I knew prejudice existed, but I didn't have to face it. Then the Nazis decided to invade my neighborhood.

The Jewish community organized a counter-demonstration to

be held at the lakefront, and our rabbi urged us to go there. "Don't give the Nazis the satisfaction of seeing a large crowd," he said. "Protest by coming to the counter-demonstration."

I knew he was right, but I also knew I had to go to the Nazi speech. Less than a mile from my house, they were going to make speeches about killing Jews. I couldn't let them do that without trying to stop them. I didn't know how—perhaps simply by yelling—but I knew I had to do something. I didn't feel violent or full of hate. I just didn't want them to speak. I thought of my father who used to share with us a faded newspaper clipping about how he was arrested for breaking up a Bund meeting in the late thirties. I was sure he would have been proud of me.

It was sunny, bright fall day. The park had a '60s feel. Groups clustered together: Jewish groups, communist groups, black groups, feminist groups, and even an environmental rights awareness group. They waved signs: "Remember the Holocaust," "Never again," "Nazis hate blacks, too," "Equality is genderless," "Save the whales." There was singing and dancing. I participated in more than one *hora,* the Jewish ring dance most people associate with weddings. The feminists were singing "We Shall Overcome." A vendor wandered through the throng, selling balloons and American flags.

Some men with official tags were roaming the crowd, giving instructions. A short man wearing a skullcap approached me. "Remember, no violence. Yell and scream when they begin to speak, but nobody should get hurt."

When he moved on, I noticed that a large guy, about 6'3" and 220 pounds, was staring at the short man with contempt. The big man glanced at me. "No violence, bullshit. That's what Jews used to say." He yelled after the guy, "Did they say non-violence in Warsaw? in Jerusalem?"

He turned to me again. "I tell you what I'm going to do. When they start speaking, I'm going to rush them and kill them with my hands." He held up his hands so I could see them. "That's what I'm going to do." He shook my hand. "I'm Izzy. Remember what I said." Then he wandered off. I thought to myself that there had to be a few nuts in this kind of crowd.

Evanston police were everywhere. Their squad cars lined the entire block adjacent to the park. Police helicopters buzzed overhead. And then the state riot police arrived. Perhaps fifty policemen exited a bus and formed themselves in two rows. They marched toward us like Roman gladiators, carrying shields and billy clubs and wearing helmets with plastic visors that covered their whole faces. As they marched, they swung their billy clubs up and down in perfect precision.

The police had cordoned off a space of about one hundred feet in front of a small maintenance building. The Nazis could park their car next to the building and would have to walk only about fifteen feet to this site to make their speech. The rope would keep people from getting too close to them and the building would protect their backs.

As the riot police reached the cordoned-off area, they formed themselves in five rows, and stood there at parade rest facing us. A man gave me a nudge. "Look at that. The police are protecting the Nazis. They should be arresting them."

I looked at the man, an old Jew, almost completely bald except for a fringe of gray hair. He was pot-bellied and bandy-legged now, but he must have been a strong man in his youth. I looked at his hands, huge hands with large square fingers.

"It's America," said the woman next to him. I assumed she was his wife. She clung to his arm.

He stood there, squeezing the rope in front of us and shaking his head. "I was in the camps," he said to me, showing me the tattooed number on his arm. "I can't believe the Nazis are going to speak in this country. Right here." He waved his arm as if to take in the whole park and shook his head in amazement.

"Believe it." She spoke to him, but she looked at me. "There are crazies all over."

"But why should they be allowed to speak?" he asked me. "In Germany they were in charge. They did whatever they wanted. But here?"

"Here!" his wife broke in. "Here we have freedom, so they are free to do what they want."

"It's a shame," he said, shaking his head again. "It's just a shame."

And then a cry went up, "They're coming." A chant began, "Nazis, no! Nazis, no!" I craned my neck and saw an old Chevy pulling up near the building. The driver's door was dented, the rear bumper had been tied on with a rope, and the car was burning oil. The Nazis were driving a junker.

I started to laugh but stopped when they got out and I saw their Nazi uniforms complete with arm bands. The sight of those uniforms sent an electrical charge through the crowd. The chant changed to "Kill the Nazis!" Kill the Nazis!" People pushed toward them, forcing us up against the rope. The old man next to me began muttering to himself, "It's happening again. It's happening again."

The Nazis marched arrogantly to a space behind the police. They smiled at one another, ignoring the crowd. Five stood at attention, while one in a black uniform stepped forward with a bullhorn. The chanting grew louder. People screamed, howled. As the Nazi began to speak, the cacophony of noise reached a crescendo, yet you could still hear him.

A few rocks and batteries began flying through the air. The speaker backed up, ducking the missiles. People cheered. A second volley filled the sky. A policeman went down, hit by a brick. Again the people cheered. The Nazi was still speaking. More things flew through the air, and then, suddenly, I saw a big man duck under the rope and begin to sprint toward the police and the Nazis. It was Izzy. A woman standing next to me began to shout, "Yes! Yes!" as if she were watching someone running for a touchdown.

Izzy made it through the first two rows of police, probably because they were stunned that anyone would try to get through. But when he reached the third row, the policemen converged on him and beat him to the ground. People began to boo. Cries of "Kill the police! Kill the pigs!" filled the air.

Then a second man charged toward the Nazis. He, too, was knocked down. Then a third, a fourth, a fifth. It was as if bits of the crowd were breaking away, drawn by the Nazis' magnetism. Indeed, the whole crowd seem to pulsate toward them, periodically crushing us against the rope. I was sure that any minute the rope would break and the entire crowd would rush the Nazis.

And still I could hear the Nazi speaking. Somehow I could hear him even clearer now, in the midst of all the screaming and chanting. It seemed as if his voice were louder, as if he had gained strength from all the hatred around him. I thought of Hitler.

Then the old man next to me shouted, "Not again! Not again!" He shook his fist at the Nazis, lifted up the rope, and started to run toward them.

His wife dove at his legs. She grabbed one and hung on. "Help me, someone help me," she shouted as her husband dragged her along the ground. "They'll kill him. Help me." He was kicking at her with one leg, fighting to get away. She must have been wearing a wig. It had come loose and I could see that she was almost as bald as her husband.

Suddenly, I ducked under the rope, but it wasn't to help her. I was running toward the Nazis. I knew that I probably wouldn't reach them, that the police would beat me to the ground, but it didn't matter. I wanted to kill them. I wanted to shove the bullhorn down the Nazi's throat. I wanted to rip out his tongue. I ran with tears in my eyes, spurred on by a kind of righteous hatred. I was going to destroy hate with hate. I was going to kill the killers.

I was about fifteen feet from the police when the Nazis started to retreat to their car. Instead of clubbing me, the first policeman I reached grabbed me in a bear hug. "Hey, they're going," he yelled, getting right up into my face. "Take it easy. They're going."

And then, just like that, it was over. I saw the Nazis being hustled into their Chevy, blue smoke pouring out of the exhaust as they pulled away. The people cheered and then quickly began to disperse. The riot police formed and marched off as if this had been a routine outing.

The next day the newspapers would write the story up as if it had been a victory—the Nazis had been stopped from speaking. But I didn't feel like a victor. As I stood there shaking with adrenaline, I thought of violence that had been in my heart and of all the brutality that had taken place. I knew that hatred had been the only victor on this day.

After the Nazis left, the park looked like a battlefield. Two ambulances had pulled up next to the injured, their swirling lights bathing the scene in blue and red. Izzy was propped up against the building. Blood ran down his face. Other people lay spread out on the ground while paramedics worked on their wounds.

The old man was still seated on the grass, his legs forming a little circle in front of him. Dirt crusted his face. His wife held him and smoothed his forehead again and again as he stared into space. I noticed that her wig was still crooked. "Shhh, it's over," she said softly. "It's over. It's over."

The Whole Megillah

I felt as if I were starring in a Jewish version of *Father Knows Best.* The Sabbath table was loaded with food, a cornucopia of chicken, asparagus, potatoes, and salad. The light from the Sabbath candles flickered warmly. Adrienne and Sarah were discussing dolls. Zach was telling me about a collage he wanted to make. We could have been posing for a Norman Rockwell painting. Then the phone rang, ruining the perfect moment. "Damn," I exploded.

Both kids immediately ended their conversations and began a sing-song chant, "ooo … ooo," "ooo … ooo."

"Daddy swore," yelled my seven-year-old son, pointing at me and looking at his mother.

"That's a bad word, Daddy," admonished his nine-year-old sister.

Seeing that I was caught red-handed (or in this case red-worded), Adrienne suggested that we make a game of it. Everyone would get to say one swear word.

"I'll begin," Adrienne said. She stared at the kids with a mischievous gleam in her eyes and whispered, "Hell."

We turned toward Sarah, who, when she realized it was her turn, gave us a look of terror. "I can't say it," she blurted out. She seemed ready to bolt out the door. "Why don't you write it down?" Adrienne suggested.

Sarah wrote her word with one hand cupping the paper so we couldn't peek. Then she slid the paper to Adrienne who nodded in approval and slipped it to me. I lifted the corner as if I were hoping to fill an inside straight. "Good word," I said to Sarah's chagrin.

"Let me see," Zach shouted.

"He just wants to learn another swear word," said Sarah with disdain. "He sits in the back of the school bus and spells swears with the other boys."

Adrienne and I turned toward our son. Zach leaned back in his chair, folded his arms in front of him, and said slowly, loudly, and distinctly, "A … S … S." He smiled as if he had just won the local spelling bee. Then, before we had a chance to say anything, Zach began to swear a blue streak. He only stopped to convulse in laughter because I had slapped my hand over his mouth. Sometimes life changes the channels on you. In the flick of a tongue, *Father Knows Best* had become *Married with Children.*

PURIM WAS APPROACHING. During this Jewish holiday, we read the biblical Book of Esther. The story celebrates how the Jews were saved from destruction by Esther and her uncle, Mordechai, who outwitted Haman, the Persian king's evil advisor.

The holiday is designed for children. Most synagogues hold Purim carnivals, a Jewish version of an amusement park. Social halls across the country fill with screaming children, bent on throwing bean bags through Haman's mouth or ringing Haman's upturned nose with plastic hoops.

You won't find hot dogs at these events; instead the tables are piled high with *hamantashen,* triangular-shaped cookies that are supposed to look like Haman's hat. The ones the parents bake are light and flaky; the heavy ones clunk out of the ovens of the Hebrew school classes.

The fun continues even through the Purim service when we read the Book of Esther. Whenever Haman's name is mentioned, the children whirl *greggers,* noise makers that sound like cicadas gone mad.

Everyone comes to the service in costume to march in the costume parade. Mordechais walk in wearing cotton beards, real beards, and no beards at all. Hamans come in every shape and size, many sporting penciled-in evil-looking moustaches, curled at the ends. Comely Esthers wrap themselves in oversized slips and arrive weighted down with costume jewelry.

But people can dress up as anything, not just as characters from the story. We always get a slew of oddball costumes. Once, in an ecumenical spirit, we even hosted the Pope. One of our congregants resembled the man, so he came dressed in elegant robes, looking as if he had just stepped off the pages of *Newsweek.* When he arrived, someone greeted him with, "Good *Yontiff* (holiday), Pontiff."

Even our rabbi takes part. Once he and his wife wore gray sweat suits with little cotton tails sewn on the back. They were no longer rabbi and rebbitsin, but now rabbit and rabbitsin. Another time the rabbi showed up in a Superman outfit, but he had a CS emblazoned on his chest and he carried a big soup pot. He explained that he wasn't Superman but Chicken Souperman.

Our family never had any trouble getting dressed for Purim. When the kids were younger, they fit the stereotypes for girl and boy. Destined to be Esther, baby Sarah loved sitting in the middle of the living room, quietly putting blocks together. She was always so calm. We thought that we were wonderful parents.

Then Zach came along and taught us humility. Baby Zach would run into a room, hit a wall, bounce off with a grin, and keep going.

As she got older, Sarah became involved in rhythmic gymnastics and improvisational drama. In the morning, we were never sure if she would spring into the kitchen like Mary Lou Retton or slink in like Sarah Bernhardt. Zach's preferred activities were break dancing and karate. He acted like someone out of a hip kung fu movie.

While Sarah made clothes for her Cabbage Patch doll, Zach carried around a box full of little plastic cars and trucks called Transformers. When you twisted, turned, and tugged them, they became robot monsters that bore names like Voltran, Megatron, Maladroid, Decepticon, and Autobot. One day when I complained that he was spending too much time with these toys, Zach looked at me in astonishment and said, "Dad, you don't know it, but at this very moment, the Autobots are protecting the earth from the Decepticons."

So when Purim came along, Sarah would drape one of Adrienne's old nightgowns around her. Then she'd add makeup, dangling earrings, and a veil.

Of course, Zach always wanted to be Haman. The transformation would take place by means of a robe and a towel twisted to look like a turban. I would burn some cork and smudge a mustache and beard on his evil little Haman face.

I usually dressed as a larger version of Haman, but Adrienne never dressed like Esther. She's a feminist, so she likes to dress as Vashti, the King's first wife who refused to dance for him and his cronies. She'd don an old robe, put her hair up in rollers, and carry a sign that read, "Not tonight, dear, I have a headache."

One night right before Purim, as we were finishing dinner, Adrienne said, "Why don't we try new costumes for Purim this year? We always dress the same way."

"But I want to be Esther," Sarah whined.

"And I want to be Haman," I mimicked.

We all looked at Zach.

"I want dessert," he said.

Adrienne shrugged, realizing that this wasn't the right moment for innovation.

But the next night Adrienne again brought up the idea of new Purim costumes. From the look on her face, I knew that she wasn't about to be deterred. "Let's see what costumes the kids want to wear. You go ask Zach and I'll talk to Sarah."

"Thanks for the easy job," I replied. "And what if he picks something crazy?" Once for Halloween he dressed up as Michael Jackson in black parachute pants, the shiny kind with about forty zippers; a red baseball jacket; and green ropes tied around his arms. He slicked his hair back with water and donned a pair of shades. Paper clips hung down from one side of the sunglasses, Michael Jackson key chains from the other.

"Bargain with him," she said.

Oh, sure, I thought. Bargaining with Zach was like bargaining with my father, the used car salesman. When Zach discovered that I had recorded a story about him, he demanded royalties because he had heard that I was paying an author for rights to record his story. I thought, how cute, and agreed to pay him two cents a cassette. I didn't know then that I was creating a monster.

For the next few days he pestered Adrienne and me about his earnings every chance he got. Adrienne grew so tired of it, she cornered me in the kitchen and growled, "Buy him out."

So Zach and I sat down around the kitchen table to negotiate our new business deal. "How much do you want for the story?" I asked, getting right down to business.

Zach folded his arms and leaned back in his chair. Then, as if he were offering me a close-out special or presenting me with an unheard-of-bargain for a limited amount of time, he looked me in the eye and said, "Ten dollars, but that's the price today. Tomorrow it goes up." I took the deal.

Zach sat in his room amid a wasteland of scattered Lego blocks and dirty clothes, intent on some intergalactic battle. Before I could bring up the subject of costumes, Zach said, "Dad, they have something better than hot lunch at school." Adrienne always packed nutritional lunches for school, but every now and then when she was too busy she'd give the kids money to buy hot lunch. Of course, they loved hot lunch. I was surprised to hear that there was something better.

"What's that?" I asked, sitting down on the floor.

"They call it *à la carte*," he whispered conspiratorially. Zach quickly looked by me to see if Adrienne, the high priestess of food, was in the area. When he saw she wasn't, he leaned toward me and said in a voice filled with wonder, "Dad, you can get anything you want. Today, I got spaghetti, chips, and a dessert, and they gave me change." My son had found junk food heaven, and he had also pocketed the change.

"Zach," I said, deciding to deal with nutrition and money matters later, "Mom really wants to go to the Purim carnival in new costumes this year. If you had your choice, what would you go as?"

"A Decepticon," he said without hesitation.

"So?" I asked when I met Adrienne downstairs.

"Well, Sarah doesn't want to change costumes but if we really, really want her to, she's willing to dress as whatever we want but she hopes she'll be beautiful. How about Zach?"

"He wants to destroy the world."

Adrienne decided to take matters into her own hands. She sprang her idea on us at dinner the next night. "Why don't we go as the Megillah?" she asked in a hopeful tone. In Hebrew the word means scroll, but it is also used to describe the story itself, so I was baffled. The kids looked mystified, too. "You kids will go as the little Megillah. Dad and I will be the big Megillah."

"What are you talking about, Dear?" I asked gently.

"It'll be great," Adrienne began in her best sales voice. "I'll print some of the story of Esther onto butcher paper. Then we'll roll the ends of the paper around us. So we'll be the poles. The story will spread between us." She waved her hand in front of her by way of explanation. "I know there's only one pole in the original—it just unwinds—but who will care?"

Sarah poked at her potatoes, unsure what this idea had to do with beauty. Zach had suddenly decided to demolish some peas.

Besides the fact that the Megillah has only one post, Adrienne's idea had a serious flaw—putting Zachary and Sarah, Haman and Esther, a boy and a girl, into the same costume.

They began to fight as soon as we rolled the paper on them. "You're wearing the paper too high," shouted Zach.

"No, I'm not." said Sarah, dripping condescension. "You're wearing it too low."

"Mom, Sarah's got too much paper," Zach yelled.

"No, I don't," said Sarah in the snotty tone that only older sisters can manage. "It's you that has too much."

"Let's hurry up," Adrienne said to me, "and get them to the synagogue. Once the costume parade starts, they'll be fine."

I stowed our costume in the trunk and opened the back door of the car for Sarah and Zach to slide in. Sarah gave me a look of exasperation. "You know, we're not going to be able to sit down," she said.

"But I want to sit down," Zach whined.

"Just get in the car and stand in the back," Adrienne ordered. "It takes only a few minutes to get to the synagogue."

"I want to sit down," Zach repeated once he was in the car.

"Then sit," said his sister.

"But I can't if you don't."

"Well, I don't want to ruin the costume."

"Mom," shouted Zach.

"Mom," shouted Sarah.

They fought all the way to the synagogue and they fought all the way through the reading of the Megillah. They weren't even happy when they spun their noisy *greggers.*

I thought that once the parade started they would be fine. I had actually begun to like the new costumes. They were easily the most creative in the sanctuary, and when we had entered we had received approving laughter. I leaned toward Adrienne, who seemed to be growing more depressed the longer the kids argued.

"It's going to be all right. They'll be fine when everyone starts to admire their costume."

We lined up to march around the synagogue. The kids were right in front of us, glowering at each other. In front of them was the matzo ball family, father and sons stuffed into yellow costumes designed to look like matzo balls. Actually, they resembled dumpy pumpkins. The mother followed in a baseball uniform, swinging a baseball bat. Behind us was a woman dressed in green tights, green sweater, green hat and a colorful collar. "Who are you?" I asked.

"Why, Queen Aster," she replied.

As soon as we started marching, the battle began again.

"You're walking too fast," Sarah complained. "Slow down." Zach didn't answer. He had realized something important—that Sarah was attached to him as much as he was attached to her. He began to speed up.

"Dad," yelled Sarah over her shoulder, looking as if she were on a runaway train. But there was nothing I could do. Zach was the engine.

"Go left," Sarah shouted, as they came to the end of the aisle. After all, that's where the parade was headed. Zach turned right, striking out on his own.

This was too much for Sarah. "Zachary, stop this instant," she screamed. Then she stopped. Zach jerked back like a fish on a hook. For a second he stopped and stared at Sarah in anger. Then an idea came to him. He smiled at her and at us, turned and ran at full speed. Sarah dug in her heels and the paper ripped right in two.

We had to console Sarah with some *hamantashen,* but soon she ran off to play with her friends. Zach happily ran up and down the aisles, his portion of the Megillah trailing behind him like a banner. He charged up to us. "Great costume, Mom," he said. "Let's do it again next year." Then he was off, flying around the outside of the synagogue, his friends chasing after him, as if he were rallying them in the Decepticon's eternal battle against the Autobots.

Sarah and Mopsy

Our daughter Sarah is a junior at Harvard. We've missed her a lot since she left for college, but this year was the worst: she took a job in Massachusetts and didn't even come home for the summer. Adrienne went down to the basement and dragged up an 11" x 14" picture of Sarah that we had mounted on a board long ago. She propped it in Sarah's bedroom doorway, so that every time we walked by her room, we could say "hi" to our daughter.

The picture shows Sarah at the tender age of twelve, sitting on her bed. She's smiling through her braces and hugging a stuffed rabbit to her chest ....

"BUT I CAN'T GO," said Sarah. I traded glances with Adrienne. The three of us were sitting at the kitchen table discussing the fifth-grade overnight camping trip.

"What do you mean you can't go?" I asked.

"I just can't," she said with a heightened tone of exasperation. "What if I lose Mopsy?"

Mopsy was Sarah's stuffed rabbit, the companion she had slept with since she was two years old. Originally, Mopsy's colors were yellow and white. But now, she was a dirty gray. The little cape with "Mopsy" written on it had disappeared long ago. The ears had fallen off and one had been sewn on backwards. But we weren't talking looks here. We were talking the Velveteen Rabbit.

The summer before, we had taken a camping trip out West. On our first night camping in the Grand Tetons, Sarah discovered she had left Mopsy in Yellowstone. She looked at us seriously. "We have to go back," she said. "We have to."

I didn't know how to reply. I pictured Mopsy being tossed in the air by Old Faithful or floating in one of those bubbling paint pots. I wasn't sure if we would ever find her, but I promised to call the park the next morning. All night in the tent, Sarah wept mournfully.

I called just after dawn, and, astonishingly, they had Mopsy. So I took off, driving the seventy-five miles to Yellowstone. That day, I drove 150 miles round trip on a two-lane highway for a bunny rabbit, but it was the best trip I ever made, because I was a hero and I knew it. And when I got back, I got a hero's hug.

Later on the trip, Sarah left Mopsy in the valley of Yosemite. "Dad," she said, looking at me very sheepishly. She didn't have to say more.

"Mopsy," I said. Sarah just shook her head, tears already forming in her eyes. This time we had the bunny sent up to our campground by bus. That afternoon, we were sitting at the local bus station when the Yosemite shuttle pulled up. An old black couple got off. A bunch of teens hopped aboard. I stuck my head in the door. "Is there a bunny on the bus?" Some passengers gave me strange looks, but the driver smiled, reached behind him, and pulled out the plastic bag that contained Mopsy. Sarah ran by me and gathered her in.

"BUT YOU CAN'T LOSE MOPSY," I said, getting up and looking in the refrigerator for something to drink. "It's not like last summer when we were traveling around."

"You'll be fine," said my wife as she cut up vegetables for a salad. "Just leave her on your bed."

"You don't understand," Sarah shouted. "You just don't understand." And with that, she rushed from the table and ran up the stairs to her room. My wife and I looked at each other in bewilderment as we heard the door slam above us.

There was a lot of slamming doors and dramatic rushing around in our house in those days. You see, a major metamorphosis had taken place in Sarah's life, a great transformation had occurred. I can put it in one word. She had become a *preadolescent.*

A notice from her school called the age "transescence." It's not in the dictionary, but it's a great word. Transescence sounds as if it means between essences, and that perfectly described Sarah at eleven.

She was still a wonderful kid. That year she got all A's in school. She read *Gone with the Wind*, and as soon as she finished it, she began plowing through it again because she loved it so much. Her doll collection numbered over a hundred and she had been saving for two years to buy an antique doll. As soon as she learned to knit, she knit a sweater for her mother. That's the kind of girl she was.

But once transescence set in, Sarah also became completely flaky. Losing Mopsy twice in one summer trip was just a harbinger of what was to come. Take her room for instance. In her old, simple childhood days, it had been a charming little room, complete with fairies dancing on the wallpaper and pictures of cats. She had an armoire for her dresses, a little desk at which to do homework, bookshelves for her dolls and books, a captain's bed with drawers underneath for her clothes. The room was idyllic: sweet, cute, and neat.

But with the onset of transescence Sarah's room began to look as if a hurricane had hit. I approached the room the way the guards approached Level Three in the movie *Aliens.* I didn't know what I'd find when I got there. It could be year-old candy in the corner. If Sarah wanted to find something to wear, she had to do an archaeological dig through the mounds of clothes on the floor. Her desk was a mess. Her bed was unmade. Her drawers were open, and the few remaining clothes in the drawers were trying to get out. They spilled over the sides in balled-up shapes, looking like those warnings explorers get in grade-B movies: "Bwana, do not enter here!" I wouldn't dare go near her drawers.

Her desk looked like a deranged Stonehenge. Piles of things loomed everywhere. You could pull anything out of that melange: *Clan of the Cave Bear* and *Little Women,* combs and dirty socks, old McDonald's game cards and molars that the dentist pulled out, used Kleenex and crumpled-up notes from school that never reached us. The kicker? On her door hung a message board with an eternal message scrawled across it. "Things to do before going out to play: clean up my room." Every now and then she penned another note, this to her long-suffering mother:

Dear Mom,

Don't worry. I'll clean up my room tomorrow.

Love,
Sarah

Once, Sarah's friend Emily wrote underneath it:

P.S. Tomorrow never comes.

Sarah's room had become a wasteland, a no-man's land, a cavity in the tooth of her parents' existence. It had turned into a strange cocoon into which my little daughter stepped one day and out flew a flaky eleven-year-old.

Is it any wonder that she was worried about losing Mopsy on the camping trip? It was surprising that she hadn't lost Mopsy in her bedroom.

I went upstairs, hoping to calm Sarah, but when I entered her room, I remembered how short the transescent attention span was.

Sarah had already moved on to other matters. I found her with twelve dots of Noxzema on her face. I said, "Sarah, it looks as if you are going on the warpath."

"D-a-a-a-a-d!" she yelled. "D-a-a-a-a-d! "That's the transescent chant—one syllable elongated and overflowing with disdain. Translated, it means, "You're so impossible!"

It really was as if Sarah had joined some primitive tribe and was going through a rite of passage. For instance, there was the clothing ritual. We had thought that the problem of Sarah throwing her clothes on the floor would solve itself. After all, she had always liked to be neat when she went to school. We didn't know that for transescents wrinkled was in. Sarah was using the floor to make her clothes more attractive the way we would use an ironing board—she was trampling in the wrinkles.

And sloppy! She called it baggy. I had thought that she would grow up and wear her mother's clothes. Instead, she grew up to wear mine. She would march into my closet and claim my T-shirt, my shirt, my sweater. Then she would wear them all, one on top of the other.

Thank God, the latest fashion at the high school hadn't yet reached the junior high. In the high school the girls were wearing men's boxer underwear for shorts. I have a colleague whose daughter was a senior at that time. He said to me, "Syd, you haven't experienced anything until you've seen your underwear walking down a school hall."

And bizarre! Sarah had bought a black coat at a thrift shop to wear when she played Charlie Chaplin in a school play. Soon she began wearing it to school every day with a black hat. My wife said, "She has such style." But to me, she looked like a Hasidic Jew or an Amish farmer.

The worst occurred one morning when she donned a dress she used to wear for dress-up when she was little. It was an old, gauzy, blue prom dress. Over it she pulled one of my L.L. Bean wool sweaters. She resembled a bag lady. I said, "Sarah, you're not going to school looking like that."

"D-a-a-a-a-d!" she screamed. "D-a-a-a-a-d!"

The painful part of the rite of passage also happened the year Sarah turned eleven. In primitive countries, they scar their children. In America we put braces on them. Sarah complained bitterly. She thought she looked ugly, and the "pronks," as she called them, were hurting her teeth. Of course, her brother Zach called her "metal mouth."

The only thing that made Sarah happy was when a teacher told her that it was better to have braces now than later when she wanted to kiss the boys. That made her happy; it didn't make me happy.

But looks weren't on Sarah's mind as the camping trip approached. She had a much bigger problem: the threat of losing Mopsy. So she decided to find a substitute sleeping partner. One night she lay down with a striped tiger hand puppet with one eye missing. The next she tried a koala bear with a white ribbon on its head. She even auditioned a huge lion named Harris. On Thursday, she found the winning candidate: a tiny mouse that was ancient enough to have the same texture as Mopsy. With the crisis averted, Sarah could go on the camping trip.

The big day came. I started to go off to work and yelled upstairs, "Have a great time at camp, Sarah."

"Dad, wait!" she cried. "Wait!" She came running down the stairs and looked at me with disbelief. "I'm going to camp, Dad. Give me a hug." So I hugged her; it was as if I had never hugged her before. This was a going-off-to-war hug.

My mind split in two there on my front porch. Right then I experienced the epitome of transescence, this age between burping and boys, between diapers and drugs. I could see the little girl in her and also the woman she was going to become.

I was hugging my little girl, the one who was worried that she couldn't sleep without her favorite bunny. But I was also hugging a future Sarah. The moment embodied all the good-byes to come. She was going off to college and I wouldn't see her for months. She was getting married and moving to another part of the country. She was taking a job in another part of the world.

I expected background music to start from *Fiddler on the Roof*: "Sunrise, sunset .... Sunrise, sunset ...." And then she was out of my arms and on her way to school and the camping trip.

When she returned a week later, I asked after the tiny mouse. She looked at me as if I was crazy and just shrugged. "No problem," is all she said and then headed toward the phone. She seemed taller and older.

And so we muddled our way toward adolescence. Sarah's room grew even messier. The phone line began to seem like her umbilical cord. She devoured *Seventeen* magazines from cover to cover. She would put conditioner in her hair, then come out of the shower and sit for half an hour before washing it out. The teen years seemed only a rinse and set away.

And then, when Sarah was twelve, Mopsy got thrown out by mistake. Mopsy had developed a large rip and Adrienne asked Sarah to put her next to the sewing machine. The woman who cleaned our house was surprised when I called.

"Yes, I threw the bunny out," she said when I called her. "It was torn, no?"

No one even noticed Mopsy was missing until long after the garbage had been picked up. I didn't think it would be a problem since Sarah was no longer sleeping with Mopsy every night. But when Sarah discovered the loss, she cried as if a family member had died. Adrienne and I tried to comfort her that night, but she was inconsolable.

The next morning when I entered her room, Sarah was still weeping. She turned toward the wall with her head buried in the pillow. "Sar," I said softly as I sat down on her bed. "Why don't we go out and buy another bunny rabbit?" She didn't respond, so I shook her gently. "Come on, Sar, it's Saturday. We'll spend the day. What do you say?" She moved away from my touch and mumbled something onto her pillow. "I can't hear you," I said.

"You don't understand," she repeated. "It won't be like Mopsy. It won't look like Mopsy. It won't smell like Mopsy."

"No problem," I replied. "I'll take care of that. I'll rip off an ear and sew it on backwards. I'll jump on it a few times. I'll wash it twenty times. I'll roll it in the dirt." I could see a little smile on her face. "Come on, Sar, you don't have to buy anything. Let's just go look."

And so we began a long day that took us from Herdrich's Variety store to Toys-R-Us. It seemed as if we visited every toy store in Chicago's northern suburbs. I thought it would be simple. There had to be lots of Mopsies out there. After all, everyone loves Beatrix Potter. But while we found bears and whales and giraffes and generic bunnies, Mopsy was nowhere to be seen.

We both grew more and more dejected as the day wore on. So over a McDonald's lunch I decided to get Sarah thinking about something else. It was a welcome change for both of us. "Sarah," I asked, "what do you want to be when you grow up?"

She paused with a French fry in mid-air and tilted her head in thought. "A teacher, a psychiatrist, or a paleoanthropologist," she replied with complete conviction.

Over that lunch, I also found out that Sarah wanted to reside in Massachusetts, near both the ocean and a large urban area. She pictured herself living in a farmhouse with lots of animals, especially cats, and, "of course," a horse. She planned on having five children—all girls. Their names were going to be Catherine,

Jocelyn, Madeleine, Megan, and Rifka.

I felt good sitting there and chatting with my daughter because I realized that transescence hadn't taken anything from me. In fact, it had brought me more. She was still my little girl. I could still sit on her, pretend I didn't see her, and complain about how lumpy the couch was. I've been playing that game with her since she was a toddler. But now we could also go out to a lunch and chat about her future.

I was lost in my reverie when Sarah said, "Don't you think we should be going?" Then she slurped down the remainder of her Coke, jumped off her seat, and headed toward the car.

Late in the afternoon, we arrived at Rosie's, a small toy store in our home town of Evanston. It looked like any number of other toy stores. Its windows held a welter of things: bright plastic gardening tools, colorful kites, board games, and two huge Raggedy Ann dolls.

Inside, the store was divided into neat little sections. The store held a book alcove, a game and puzzle corner, an area for train sets, and an entire wall of dolls. Stuffed animals were sprinkled all about. I saw Babar and Curious George, Paddington and the Velveteen Rabbit, but no Mopsy.

A woman approached us and asked if she could help. When Sarah told her what had happened, the woman replied, "This is very serious. Please come with me."

Leaving me behind, Rosie's owner led Sarah to a nook at the back of the store. "Sit right down," she said, "and tell me all about Mopsy while I make us some chamomile tea."

And so Sarah sipped her tea and poured out her heart. The woman listened with great concentration. Finally, she said, "I think I have something for you. I'll just be a minute." With that, she disappeared into the store's basement. Sarah looked at me quizzically. I shrugged my shoulders.

When the woman emerged from the basement, she held in her

hands a brand-new Mopsy. I turned to Sarah, expecting to see joy on her face. Instead I saw a look of terror.

Sarah seemed frozen as she stared at the bunny in the woman's arms. Then she spun toward me with tears in her eyes and gasped, "I can't. I just can't." Until then I hadn't realized the depth of her attachment to Mopsy.

"It's OK," I said. "It's OK, Sar." I reached out and she ran into my arms. "We don't have to buy it. It's OK. We don't have to buy anything." We hurriedly left with Sarah leaning on me, sobbing.

That night, as Sarah lay in bed, I couldn't help but think what a mixture my daughter was: so childlike, feeling all that grief over a stuffed animal; so adultlike, feeling all that love and loyalty. And I knew then that I couldn't help her. She was leaving her childhood behind, and that involved pain.

The next morning Sarah came down to breakfast and announced that she wanted to buy the new bunny. As we entered the store, the woman broke into a smile and reached below the counter. "I've been saving her for you," she said.

Sarah took the bunny in her arms, crushed it against herself, and buried her face in it. She hugged her new bunny all the way home.

LATER THAT DAY, we took the picture of Sarah that Adrienne propped in the doorway to get us through this lonely summer: there's our daughter, on the brink of adolescence, smiling and hugging her brand new bunny rabbit. She named her Rosie.

Let's Twist Again

A little north of the Lincoln Park Zoo in Chicago, a section of Lincoln Avenue has been yuppified. In a four-block area, you'll find a heavy concentration of cafes, pottery shops, health food stores, chic boutiques, and trendy bars. It was in one of these bars, Juke Box Saturday Night, that I decided to celebrate my forty-fourth birthday.

It was billed as a 1950s bar and it had a real '50s feel. Huge cutouts of Mickey Mouse and Superman hung from the ceiling. Frankie and Annette, in a scene from one of their beach blanket movies, stared at each other in a mural on one wall. On another hung a painting of a '50s drive-in, all tail fins and couples necking. Black and white television sets scattered around the place played reruns of *Leave it to Beaver* and *Dennis the Menace.*

But the best part of the bar was the D.J. who spun the platters and hyped the hula hoop contest that was to be held later. His hair curled moodily down his forehead. He wore a leather jacket and blue jeans, and he stood behind the hood and windshield of what looked as if it had been the driver's seat of a pink '57 Chevy convertible.

It was just what I needed, a night of pizza, beer, and nostalgia, especially nostalgia. It had been a hard year. Arthritis struck for the first time and getting up in the morning began to feel like a game of Russian roulette. I never knew which joint would hurt me the most.

When I first felt it, I thought I had injured myself exercising. I told an older friend as we were dressing for a workout at the club.

"It's your wrist that hurts?" he asked.

"Yeah, my wrist, and I don't remember doing anything to it. Last week my knee was hurting and I didn't even work out that much? Isn't that odd?"

He smiled. "Welcome to the club," he said. He didn't mean the one we were standing in.

During the year, I began to go gray, too. You can't know what that meant to me. For years I watched myself go bald. As a teenager I had a crew cut. It fit my high school, all-American image: football player, editor of the school newspaper, King of the Senior Prom. I was even voted "Most Likely to Succeed."

Then hairs started to do kamikaze leaps into the sink and my forehead began to look like Yosemite's El Capitan. When I smiled at a pretty girl on the street, she'd look at me as if I were a dirty old man. At class reunions, I was the guy who drew whispers: "Look how Lieberman's aged." It made me feel as if not only my hair, but my best years, were behind me.

Some women say that bald is beautiful but I don't really believe it. They usually have a tone in their voice that translates as, "Isn't he cute?" It's as if they were talking about a baby or a chimpanzee. I'll believe it when the next James Bond is bald.

I considered a hairpiece but I couldn't get over my childhood image of them. In those days, most hairpieces looked as if they had been bought at a neighborhood drug store or thrown in as a bonus for buying a washing machine at Polk Brothers. "And if you purchase our machine today, we will include the top of the line Aladdin hairpiece in any one of six different designer colors." They don't call them rugs for nothing.

I even visited a hair transplant doctor once. He must have been used to dealing with rich people because he promised me that "for the mere price of a Cadillac," I would look like Frank Sinatra. I could imagine buying the Cadillac but I couldn't imagine spending that much on a spotty layer of hair. Plus, the pictures of them putting the plugs in made me feel a little queasy. All I could think of was my daughter's dolls' heads. How would I explain to her what they were doing to me?

Once I was finally bald, I got used to it. I took on a new role model, trading in Robert Redford for Robert Duvall. I secretly sniggered at men with hair, thinking of what they were eventually going to face.

But going gray meant the whole aging process had started all over again. I met a woman I hadn't seen in years.

"Nancy," I yelled.

"Gray!" she replied, slapping a hand to her cheek and getting all wide-eyed. She meant old.

I knew it wouldn't get better. All my uncles on my mother's side eventually had fringes of pure white hair surrounding their bald heads.

But even worse than getting arthritis and turning gray was that during the past year I had begun to fight the weight wars. Adrienne said it was because I sneaked into the pantry too often to even out the edges of things. A snip of pizza here, a sliver of pie there. Can I help it if I like my food neat?

But the real problem was my metabolism. Ah, to be a kid again when I could eat anything I wanted. How I longed for the days before I gave up ice cream for frozen yogurt, those carefree days when I didn't read labels, looking for the percentage of calories due to fat. I would spoon peanut butter right out of the jar. I'd scarf down whole pints of ice cream from those square cardboard containers. I could eat a whole dinner at home—chicken soup, chicken, potatoes, bread, a vegetable, salad, and an apple slice for dessert—and then go to Adrienne's house and eat another entire dinner. Midnight would find me raiding the refrigerator looking for more food. And I never gained a pound.

Watching my eleven-year-old son eat brought those days back to me. The summer before I'd taken him to a Cubs game. On the way there, he devoured a McDonald's hamburger and fries. In the first inning, he bolted down a hot dog. Two innings later, he inhaled a piece of pizza. By the fifth, he had a taste for nachos. In the seventh, he had moved on to peanuts. And for the ninth, he decided on ice cream. Thank God the game didn't go into extra innings. On the way home, he asked, "What's for dinner? I'm starving."

You see, Zach's metabolism ovens were going full tilt. He had these big, brawny workmen shoveling in the calories. Me? I had one worker. A little guy. He must have worked for the Teamsters because he took a lot of breaks. Every now and then, he remembered to throw in half a load.

Yet I still attempted to stay in shape. First, I tried aerobics. That's an experience for a man in his mid-forties. There were always about fifty young women in the class, lithe college students in skintight leotards, doing complicated kick-and-twist routines. They looked as if gravity didn't apply to them as they bounced and ran tirelessly.

Then there were usually four middle-aged guys like me in baggy sweat pants and unmatched sweatshirts, bumping into each other and stumbling into the girls. As we tried to keep up with routines, we looked a lot like bears trudging through mud.

The instructor was always so full of energy and good cheer, whooping and talking and joking as she breezed through the exercises. "How do you feel?" she would inevitably shout. "Good," the girls would yell back as they kicked over their heads or leaped through the air. I couldn't get enough breath to even attempt an answer.

So I began to jog, my new belly bouncing under my old sweats, my joints hurting. Young men plugged into Walkmans loped by me as if I were standing still. Young girls in color-coordinated leotards and tights floated by, chattering as they went. When I passed some old geezer doing his power walk, I could see my future. I wanted to yell at him for going so slowly; I wanted to run him off the road.

I had played halfback on my high school football team. I'm a little guy—5' 6" 1/2—so whenever I scored a touchdown in a high school football game, the newspapers would write, "Lieberman scampers into the end zone." It always made me feel like a squirrel. But if someone were writing about my jogging, he wouldn't have used the verb "scampered." He would more likely have written, "Lieberman chugs down the street." And I no longer felt like a squirrel; I was more like the African Queen.

But the worst thing about the year leading up to my forty-fourth birthday was that Sarah turned thirteen, the age Adrienne was when I first met her. How had that happened? A second ago I was rocking Sarah in my arms trying to get her to sleep, and suddenly she was slow dancing in some boy's arms. A second ago she had followed me around the house. But at thirteen she was so busy with friends, I couldn't ever find her. A second ago everything I said had been wise and every joke I told hilarious. Then I became incredibly stupid and terminally boring.

So you can see why I needed a night of nostalgia, a night to feel young again. And it was working. I felt younger, thinner, hairier. I was sitting there pleasantly musing and sipping my light beer when I felt a tap on my shoulder. I turned and found myself staring at a young guy. He looked like a college student. "Excuse me," he said, "but is this seat taken, sir?"

SIR? SIR! ... Sir is a middle-aged man's "Mirror, mirror on the wall," reminding you of the truth. It's the bell sounding midnight in *Cinderella,* waking you from your dreams and returning you to reality. Sir is the word I would use to address my date's father, my professors. Sir is the person I give my seat to on the bus.

I was ready to fight. I slammed my beer down on the table and shouted, “How old do you think I am?”

The kid leaped back, astonished. But before he could stammer a reply, a friend of mine who was there for my birthday—someone who was older, grayer, and heavier than I—threw an arm around my shoulders, kissed me on the cheek and said, “A baby. You’re just a baby.”

It made me think of my mother. I’m the baby of the family and to this day, whenever she introduces me, she’ll say, “This is my baby.” If she’s around when I’m in my seventies, if I discover a cure for AIDS, she’ll still introduce me that way.

After my father died, she had met a man and lived with him for eleven years. They couldn’t get married because she would have lost my father’s Social Security payments. After he died, she told me, “I’m through with men.”

A few months later, I got a call. “In case you were going to call me tonight, I wanted to tell you I’m not going to be home.”

“Where will you be?” I asked.

“A friend fixed me up. I’m going out on a date.”

“I thought you told me that you were through with men,” I said.

“What is it? It’s just a date. I’m not getting married.”

A week later I got another call. “In case you were going to call me tonight, I’m not going to be home.”

“Another date, Mom?” I asked.

“My new friend is taking me to Amish country in Indiana and he said that we might not get back home tonight. We’re going to stay in a motel.”

I told Adrienne, who got hysterical. She grabbed the phone and asked, “Are you going to stay in one motel room or two?”

“One, of course,” my seventy-year-old mother replied. “Why

should we waste the money?"

Suddenly, she was seventy going on seventeen. She and her new boyfriend began to fly around like teenagers. She was never home when I called. "If only I were ten years younger, I'd really be enjoying this," she said to me. "Syd," she added, "when I wake up in the morning, I'm filled with aches and pains. But then I go to the bathroom and put on my make-up and get dressed and begin the day. Complain after you're dead. Then you'll have plenty of time."

Well, the words of my friend and the advice of my mother woke me up. I got out of my seat and threw an arm around the befuddled kid. "Son," I said, "take my seat. I've got a rug to cut."

I began jitterbugging with Adrienne. We were great. After all we were an authentic couple, having danced like this when we were fourteen and thirteen. We had all the cool spin moves down perfectly. If there had been a jitterbug contest that night we could have won it. But better than that, I began to feel as if we were kids again, when Johnny Mathis sang everything that was in your heart, when slow dancing meant hugging each other and rocking in one spot, when every look was eternal and every touch earth-shattering.

It happened while I was twisting to Chubby Checker. I was turning in a circle and suddenly right in front of me, springing up from the floor, was every man's dream of a twenty-year-old blonde. She had long hair tied back in a pony tail, blue eyes, and a beautiful figure, and she was twisting like crazy in a little halter top and hot pants. She must have been coming up from one of those up-and-down twist moves when I saw her, but for a second I thought I had conjured her up. She was like Athena leaping full-grown from Zeus's head.

I stopped dancing and my mouth fell open. I just stood there staring. Then I remembered Adrienne. I nudged her. "Can we take her home?" I asked.

And my wife of twenty-one years looked her over and replied,

"Why not?"

Then we laughed and began to twist again. From old to young and back again. Twisting like we did last summer. Twisting like we did last year. Remembering when things were really humming. Twisting again. For twisting time is here.

Zen and the Art of Storytelling

"I'm not sure if storytelling is right for this kind of event," I said over the phone.

"It's perfect," Mr. Hansen replied. There was a smile in his voice. "Family entertainment for a family event."

I was skeptical about the job. Being a salesman's son, I've developed a sense for when someone is trying to sell me something. And, after eleven years as a professional storyteller, I knew that storytelling at a company picnic carried a high potential for disaster.

"A picnic can be pretty wild," I continued. "You need a quiet space for storytelling so people can hear the words. Are you going to have a tent?"

"Of course! We're going to have a tent exclusively for performances. I'll tell you what," Hansen said, dropping his voice as if we were co-conspirators. "I'll personally make sure that they place the performance tent way off to the side, away from all the other activities."

"What else will be going on?" I asked.

"Right now, we're not sure, but it's not going to be wild. After all, it's a bank picnic," he said with a laugh.

Then he got serious again. "Listen, I'm glad you mentioned the quiet stuff. That's good. Anything else I should know?" We talked about the stage and the lighting, the kind of microphone I would need, and the time I would perform. I also asked him to publicize that the show would not be appropriate for toddlers. Hansen kept assuring me that he would do everything I asked. Against my better judgment, I agreed to do the job.

WHEN I FIRST BECAME a professional storyteller, I didn't know enough to worry about where and to whom I was telling. I began my career in 1982 by taking a weeklong storytelling class. As soon as I returned home, I inhaled deeply and marched in to see the branch librarian, two of whose kids had been my students.

"Virginia," I announced, "Not only am I a teacher, but now I'm also a professional storyteller. I want to perform at the library downtown."

Without hearing me tell one line of a story, Virginia picked up the phone and called the head of the library system in Evanston. "B.J.," she said, "I have a marvelous storyteller here. If we don't sign him up right now, we're going to lose him. Get out your calendar."

Of the hundred people in the audience, about ninety were family or friends. But I was so nervous I even worried about forgetting which stories I was going to tell. Adrienne sat in the first row holding up a sign board that listed the titles.

At the start of my career, I was grateful for any job and I wasn't too particular. I told *Beowulf* to three hundred junior high students in front of a Coke machine in a school lunchroom. I entertained at birthday parties amid ripped-up present wrapping and crying kids. I told stories around campfires, competing with smoke and some-mores. And I performed at countless synagogue sisterhood meetings on Tuesday nights. Those were my small clubs. After the minutes and motions, they served me along with the sponge cake and coffee.

Those first years produced some strange moments. I once arrived at a senior citizen center to find that the person who hired me had forgotten to notify the facility that I was coming. When I introduced myself, the receptionist stared at me blankly, then called an administrator who led me to a small, brightly-lit lounge. "I'll try to find someone," she pronounced coldly, as if performing there had been my idea.

About ten minutes later, a nurse wheeled in one resident, while three more on walkers hobbled in behind her. One senior looked wildly in all directions and periodically shouted, "Are you the lecturer?"

"Here they are," the nurse said, as if I had ordered the four residents from a menu. Three stared blankly at me. The fourth seemed on the verge of recognizing me as a long-lost relative.

In lieu of my usual introduction, I simply announced that I was a storyteller and launched into a folktale. Heading toward what I considered the dramatic conclusion of my first story, I discovered that my entire audience had fallen asleep.

It was a Zen moment: If a storyteller tells a story and no one hears it, has the story been told? I pondered what to do. Do I just keep going? Do I wake them up to listen to the rest of the story? One patient began to snore loudly. Another smiled in her sleep as if enjoying a good dream. They looked so peaceful, I knew I had been a success. "Goodnight," I whispered and tiptoed out.

But perhaps the oddest job I took in those early days was the Hollywood Bar Mitzvah. That's what the Bar Mitzvah boy's father called it when he hired me to fly to Los Angeles to perform at his son's party.

"What kinds of stories do you want me to tell?" I asked when I was being hired.

"Stories that would fit a Bar Mitzvah," he replied. "Oh, and wear a tux." The Bar Mitzvah invitation he sent came surrounded by confetti inside a plastic champagne bottle.

That Saturday morning, a thirteen-year-old boy read from the Torah for the first time. The event signaled his entry into manhood. Naturally, one would expect a celebration afterward, but who could ever have imagined a Hollywood Bar Mitzvah?

As the audience pulled up to the hotel, they were greeted by two spotlights, creating an opening-night effect. Uniformed attendants helped them out of their cars. The audience walked down a red carpet through a crowd of young girls who waved autograph books and "ooohed" and "aaahed" as if watching celebrities. Flashes kept exploding as three photographers jockeyed for the best position. When the Bar Mitzvah boy arrived, the girls rushed him as if he were a rock star, pressing him for autographs.

My performance was sandwiched between a twenty-piece band and a magic act. The band was something out of the 1940s: a lead torch singer, wearing a strapless evening gown; a band leader, smiling Lawrence Welk-like out at the audience; the musicians in powder blue tuxedos.

The magician performed card tricks with oversized cards so people could see. He needn't have worried. A television camera broadcast his tricks on several large-screen television sets placed strategically around the big hall. For his last trick, the magician pulled eggs out of the Bar Mitzvah boy's ear.

As I stood in the center of the stage in my tux, the hand-held mike in my palm, I felt more like Tony Bennett than a storyteller. Activity swirled around me. Waiters glided across the room. People ate and talked. The proud parents were table hopping. The Bar Mitzvah boy and his friends hunched around a number of video games that had been assembled in the Arcade Corner, a place identified by a blinking set of neon lights. Jewish stories seemed more than a bit superfluous.

Many of these odd bookings disappeared as my career progressed. I began to feel more like an artist. One weekend I performed at a convention held at the Fountainbleu, in Miami. My hosts picked me up in a limo and put me up in a four-room suite that included a wet bar and kitchen. At the rehearsal, the director of the event said, "I'm sure you'll want a roving spot."

"Certainly," I answered. I had arrived.

But performing with lights, a sound system, and a director made it difficult to combine storytelling with my day job as a high school English teacher. One morning when I complained to a sleepy class that people actually paid to hear me speak, one kid earnestly asked, "Why?"

SO AFTER ELEVEN YEARS in the business, I should have known enough not to accept a job at a company picnic. After all, I no longer took jobs at shopping malls where they asked me to perform next to a miniature train and a clown passing out helium balloons.

Trying to stifle my doubts, I reminded myself that Hansen had complied with everything I asked. And, as he had boasted, it was a bank picnic. By the time I arrived, I had assured myself that everything would be fine. Then I entered the grove. The bank picnic could have been sponsored by the people who had created the Hollywood Bar Mitzvah.

On my left, underneath a sign marked "Grub," picnic tables bore platters of hot dogs and hamburgers and mountains of potato salad. On my right, a calliope whined out off-key circus melodies.

The calliope provided accompaniment for the horse, camel, and elephant who marched around a pen carrying children on their backs. These hapless animals were led by shirtless, sour-faced men in vests, balloon pants, and turbans.

Wandering jugglers, mimes, and acrobats strolled through the grounds, which featured a fortune-telling tent, a face-painting tent, a haunted house, and even a tent labeled "Miniature Zoo." In front of the zoo stood a bored-looking woman with a snake wound about her neck.

Glazed with sugar and excitement, kids darted from one

activity to another. Storytelling seemed a poor relation at this feast.

But when I found Hansen, he smiled at me as if I had come for a loan. "Great that you're here," he beamed, shaking my hand. "How do you like it?" he asked, waving his arm at what looked to me like Walt Disney done by Ken Russell.

"It looks as if everyone is having fun," I answered diplomatically.

"Let me show you the performance tent," he said and started off toward a tent in the center of the grove.

Wasn't the performance tent going to be off in a corner of the field?" I asked, as I hurried behind him.

"Well, we ran into a little problem," he replied over his shoulder. "The tent for the haunted house didn't arrive, so we substituted the performance tent. We're holding the performances in the eating tent. But don't worry. It's worked out fine so far."

In the performance/eating tent a small stage faced a hundred chairs. An accordion quintet had finished performing and was packing up their instruments. Around the back a few picnic tables awaited people who preferred to eat inside.

"You're scheduled to go on at 1 P.M.," said Hansen. He checked his watch. "That's in thirty minutes.

"We have a little problem," he continued. "You got left off the schedule that we printed up and passed out to people. I was going to walk around and announce your show with a bullhorn, but my assistant forgot to bring it. I sent for another. If the bullhorn doesn't get here in time, about ten minutes before you go on, I'm going to send out messengers to stop all the activities and announce your show."

Oh sure, I thought. Great idea. "Mr. Hansen," I said, "I don't think that's wise. You don't want to force anyone to come, especially kids. They're going to be unhappy if you make them come."

"Well, then we had better hope the bullhorn gets here," he said.

When 1 P.M. rolled around and the bullhorn hadn't arrived, Hansen and I stood at the side of the stage, facing a hundred empty seats. "Well, I think you should go on anyway," he said. Before I could object, Hansen bounded onto the stage and gave me a lavish introduction.

As he finished, he began applauding and waved me onto the stage. I walked up slowly, wondering what to say.

"Mr. Hansen," I whispered, turning my back to the imaginary audience, "there's no one out there. There's no one in the audience."

He smiled at me and shook my hand. Then he turned me around and pointed at me. "Syd Liebman!" he shouted, oblivious to the fact that he had gotten my name wrong. He applauded all the way down the steps. I watched him until he left the tent. The last thing he did was flash me a thumbs-up sign.

I turned then and gazed out at the empty chairs. I scanned the few diners on the outskirts of the tent to see if they were watching, but they were too busy eating to notice me. Approaching the microphone, I thanked the imaginary audience for their imaginary applause. Then I launched into my program.

That afternoon, I did a forty-five minute set for an imaginary audience. I think they loved it. I paused at all the right times for imaginary laughter. I milked the sad moments for imaginary tears. I even indulged in a bit of between-story patter with my imaginary listeners.

Every now and then one of the eaters at the tables in the back would look up with a quizzical expression on his face, eyeing me as if I were a creature from another planet. Then he would return to his potato salad.

"Thank you," I said when I finished. "You've been a great group." Then I bowed, acknowledging their imaginary thunderous applause. "Thank you, thank you," I repeated as I waved. I considered doing an encore but decided that might be pushing it. I did blow them a few kisses as I left the stage.

About five minutes after I finished, Mr. Hansen showed up with a ethnic folk dance group in tow. "Test out the stage," he said. "I think it will be perfect for you. Perfect."

As the group clumped around, testing the wood for creaks, Hansen turned to me, and asked, "How did it go?"

"Great," I replied. "They loved it."

"Terrific," he said, pointing a finger at me. "I had the feeling that storytelling was right for this situation. Didn't I tell you?"

"You sure did," I replied.

"Let me make out your check," he said, taking a checkbook from his pocket and placing it on a speaker. "Now how do you spell Liebman?" he asked.

"With a lot of humility," I replied.

The Hospital Night from Hell

Last night at dinner, Adrienne and I laughed about how strange it is to kiss now that we are both wearing glasses. This laughter had followed a lengthy discussion of my swollen knee and her bad back. And that discussion had followed a detailed description of some stomach trouble I was having. The whole time we talked, my teenage son squinted at us in disbelief. Then he turned to his older sister, who had just arrived home from college, and said, "See what I have to put up with all year?"

I remember feeling the same way when I was his age. I couldn't believe it when my parents dissected their physical problems over dinner. Their talk made me feel as if I were eating in a doctor's office. I wondered why they were so morbid and I vowed I would never subject my kids to that. Now I know and now I do.

Some time in your forties your body starts to break down. When your eyes start to go, you have to position your head, bird-like, to be able to read anything. Soon even that doesn't help because you need longer arms.

Then you start to hear less. You wind up saying "excuse me" a lot or just pretending you hear what people are saying, smiling inanely when other people smile, nodding when they nod, and hoping you haven't just agreed to donate all your money to the Save the Yak Emergency Fund of Upper Afghanistan.

Or your joints start to give out and you have to use the treadmill at the club, joining the large-belly-and-sagging-butt group instead of jogging with the beautiful people. You no longer worry about your time in the mile but about what to read while you walk in place.

Males my age know that a visit to the doctor includes a finger up your rectum to check for prostate cancer. "Here's where we get to know one another very well," mine says with a smile. Every time.

Your teeth crack, your hair turns gray, you gain weight even while dieting. It's all pretty dismal. And one day you look in the mirror and wonder how that chubby, wrinkled-faced, bald-headed, gray-hair-around-the-fringe-eyeglass-wearing-man-with-nose-and-ear-hair got into your bathroom. It's so damn unbelievable; you just have to talk about it.

I BEGAN FEELING CHEST PAINS in the middle of the evening. That afternoon I had worked out at the health club, on both the treadmill and the Nautilus machines. I had moved from one misery-producing machine to the next as if they were stations of the cross. The last machine I used is called the Chest Press. You push two levers straight out in front of you. It's supposed to be good for the pectoral muscles.

I want to say that I was feeling really good and that's why I attached more weight to the levers than I had ever done before. Actually, a weight-lifting female who looked like Arnold Schwarzenegger was following me through the circuit of machines, and I didn't want her to think I was some kind of pansy when she went to change the weight for her turn. Once when I was seven I had been tagged out at home by a girl catcher. I still bear the emotional scars from her smirk.

Of course, I was doing more repetitions than I had ever done before. I had a nonchalant look on my face but I was straining and sweating. As I pushed the levers for my last rep, I remember thinking "You could have a heart attack doing this." I didn't tell Adrienne all that as we lay in bed. I just told her I was having a little chest pain and that I might have pulled a muscle at the club. Adrienne displayed her usual odd combination of anxiety and complacency. "You can't take chances," she said. "Your dad died from a heart attack at fifty-eight. Drive the five blocks to the emergency room and call me as soon as you get there."

"I feel silly," I replied.

"You'd feel sillier if you die."

No ambulances were roaring up to the emergency room that night; the place was empty. It had a late-night country-and-western feel: harsh neon lights, blue and red plastic chairs, a vending machine that dispensed candy and Coke, and a T.V. set that was blaring though no one watched it.

I felt absurd as I walked up to the receptionist, unsure of what to say. But she didn't even look up. She kept working on some forms as if they were the most interesting literature in the world.

Her acting that way didn't surprise me. Once in college I had gone to the emergency room because I almost sliced off a finger. Blood gushed out of it as if I had struck oil. When I approached the receptionist, she tilted her head, smiled, and asked, "What seems to be the problem?" I spilled some blood on her desk. "Oh," she said and led me to a nurse.

The nurse promptly popped a thermometer in my mouth. It seemed so motherly. I expected her to say, "My poor baby, you're sick. Let's see if you're running a temperature." I tried to point out that I was bleeding by waving the blood-soaked handkerchief. The nurse looked at me with annoyance and snapped, "We have our procedures."

As I waited there, I wondered what I could do to get this receptionist's attention. Actually, I was getting a little angry. What if this wasn't silly? What if I actually was having a heart attack? Perhaps I had minutes to live and here she was pushing around forms, acting as if I were already dead. What was she, some kind of angel of death? A moonlighter from a funeral parlor?

"Can I help you?" she finally asked.

"I'm not sure," I replied, returning to reality and remembering how foolish I felt. "Actually, I think I'm OK, but I have been feeling some pressure in my chest. A little chest pain. I don't have any other symptoms. Actually, I feel pretty good. In fact, I drove myself ...."

She raised a hand in the air. I thought she was going to tell me to stop because she couldn't listen to anything before I showed her my insurance card. I had begun to pull my wallet out of my back pocket when she pressed a button.

Suddenly, a light began flashing, bells started ringing, the doors to the inner sanctum—the emergency room—swung open, and a nurse rushed out with a wheelchair. It was like something out of a Marx Brothers movie.

The nurse circled around me and rammed the chair into the back of my knees. I fell into the seat. In an instant, we were off, banging through the doors the way you do on those ghost house rides in an amusement park. She steered me into a curtained cubicle, pushed nitroglycerin under my tongue, and took my blood pressure, while another nurse attached me to an electrocardiograph machine. I was astounded at their speed. It was like watching a crew at Indy. I expected to be thrown back out on the street in a few more seconds, good as new, and ready for the next one hundred laps.

The nitro made my head feel as if it were exploding and the electrocardiograph machine belched out sheets of waving lines. On my left a man kept moaning "Oyyy ... oyyyy ... OYYY." On my right a doctor was trying to get the details of what was bothering a woman who must have been hard of hearing.

"So what did your stool look like?" he asked.

"What?"

"Your stool. What did it look like?"

"Tool?"

"YOUR STOOL! YOUR STOOL! YOUR STOOL!"

I was praying that she wouldn't hear him.

Soon people started coming in to get my medical history and the story of what happened. One would get the information and exit. Then, as if they were partners on a wrestling tag team, another person would enter, only to ask me all the same questions. I told my history to the admitting nurse, a second nurse, a third nurse, an intern, a resident, a second resident. I thought they would never stop coming.

They acted as if I were some kind of criminal and they were trying to trip me up. Maybe I wasn't hooked up to an electrocardiograph machine at all, but a lie detector. "Aha, Mr. Lieberman, you said you were three when you had your tonsils out and now you say it was four. Get off this bed. You aren't having a heart attack, you malingerer. You're simply lying to get our sympathy."

A resident showed up who looked worse then I did. A young guy in his twenties, he had a one-day beard and dark bags under his eyes. It looked as if he had been on call for the past two hundred hours; he slumped in a chair next to me. "Well, your EKG looks good and aside from the pain in your chest, you don't have any other symptoms of a heart attack. I don't really think you are having one."

"I know it," I said. "I've been telling everyone that I'm OK. I feel absurd lying here."

"Do you think it could be gas?" he asked.

Gas? It's not that I wanted a heart attack, but gas? I could just see myself the next day telling my friends. "Man, what a night I had last night. I was in the emergency room of the hospital."

"Oh, dear, what was it? Did you break something? Was it a heart attack?"

"No, it was gas."

It would be like having hemorrhoids.

"I tell you what," he said. "Why don't you take some Maalox? Better yet, I'll take some with you. Be right back." He left my curtained area and returned with two Dixie cups filled with the white liquid. *"L'chaim,"* he said, as we chugged it down. "Listen, I'm going to have to admit you to Intensive Care even if I don't think you are having a heart attack. With your family history, it's just a precaution."

A black kid wheeled me down long halls, whose walls were sprinkled with cheery nature scenes. He wore a Walkman and bopped to a beat only he could hear. He hit everything in sight: wheelchairs, walls, people. Another orderly pushing a gurney came up next to us. The two orderlies high-fived each other and began discussing their hot dates last Saturday night. The guy on the gurney next to me shrugged his shoulders as if to say, "kids." Any minute, I expected to become an unwilling passenger in a drag race.

We entered an elevator. Oddly, it held several passengers: two doctors and three older women visiting a patient. For some reason, I had expected a private elevator to Intensive Care. The two doctors glanced at me but continued their discussion of baseball. One of the women, with some kind of animal wrapped around her neck, held a bouquet of flowers. She looked at me sadly, as if I were already in a casket and she was about to place the flowers on my chest. When the elevator stopped at my floor, she waved good-bye as I was wheeled off. I waved back.

When I arrived in Intensive Care, they attached a number of wires to my body with little suction cups, the kind you use with a toy dart gun. Soon I could see my heart on the T.V. monitor over my bed. My heart would beat, the machine would beep, and a line would rise, creating a mountain on the screen. Truly, this was interactive television. But boring.

I tried to lower my heart rate using the breathing techniques and meditation I had learned in yoga class, but I was a dismal failure. I found myself shouting, "Goddamn it, go lower," and suddenly it was as if I were staring at the Himalayan mountain range.

I studied myself: from under the hospital gown, wires headed out in all directions. I looked like Robocop in a miniskirt. When you come to the hospital, do they tell you to bring a robe or pajamas? No, they put you in those silly gowns that never close in the back. Mine had a leaf pattern and reached only to my knees. The hospital's name was printed on the top right of my frock, as if someone might actually try to steal it.

A young nurse entered, so young that she apologized for bothering me with another questionnaire. "I already told them all I know." I said. I thought of asking for a lawyer.

"No, this one is different," she replied with an earnest look on her face. I don't remember all the questions, but they certainly were different. She asked things like, "Do you shop alone?" I wasn't sure if she were interested in my physical ability or my taste in clothes. "Do you dress yourself?" If I had my pants on, I would have checked my fly. "Can you make love?" I gave her my best Valentino look and—God bless her—she blushed.

After she left, a doctor came in carrying my chart. She sat on the bed and said, "I don't think you're having a heart attack, but we don't want to take a chance because of your family history. We've done some blood tests and by morning we'll know what is happening. If your enzyme levels are elevated, it indicates muscle—perhaps heart—damage. Just get some rest and I'll see you in the morning." She patted me on the leg and left.

It was late and I managed to doze off. I imagined the beep of my heart and the leap of the line were little sheep bounding over a fence.

I didn't expect to sleep long. I knew all about those cheery nurses who barge in, flip on the lights, and wake you to take your blood pressure and temperature. They call it "taking your vitals," as if sleep isn't vital. All night long at the nurses' stations around the globe, nurses sit waiting for someone to fall asleep so they can pounce.

But it wasn't a nurse who woke me. I was sleeping soundly when suddenly I heard male voices in my room. One man was rummaging around in the drawers next to my bed. Another peered at me through the darkness. I sat bolt upright in bed, my heart beating madly, the lines swerving up and down across the T.V. screen like a car out of control. I checked the clock. It was three in the morning.

"Don't worry," said the smaller of the two men, putting his hand up to quiet me. "We're just here to get your valuables." Behind him, the large man just smiled and nodded in agreement. I thought of George and Lennie in *Of Mice and Men.*

"What?" I replied, feeling as if I were dreaming. They seemed like such polite thieves.

"Don't worry. We work for the the hospital," continued the little guy. He began to speak very slowly and loudly as if I were from another country. "WE ARE TAK-ING YOUR VAL-U-A-BLES DOWN TO THE SAFE." He motioned in the direction of the door.

I was dumbfounded. The big guy put one hand on the smaller man's shoulder and leaned toward me. He pointed at him. "He's training me," he whispered, and smiled as if that would explain everything.

"Training you? Training you on a heart patient at three in the morning! I could have had a heart attack!" When they left, the big guy turned around, smiled, and waved good-bye.

I managed to doze off but very early the next morning, a doctor and his entourage of residents swept in. The head doctor's open lab coat swirled as he wheeled into the room. Under his coat, he sported an immaculately pressed blue suit and a red-striped power tie. His temples were graying. Lean, tall, and clean shaven, he looked as if he could successfully audition for the part of Dr. Joe Martin on *All My Children.* The horde of young doctors following him looked like groupies.

The doctor scooped up my chart and began to talk to the residents. No one said a word to me.

"Excuse me," I said, "but I don't think I should be here. No one thinks that I am having a heart attack, and I feel like a damn fool. I'd like to go home."

He looked up with amazement. I wasn't sure if he was more shocked at my words or at the fact that I had deigned to address him.

He approached me the way the evil witch approached Dorothy in *The Wizard of Oz.* His face, with an evil smirk, loomed up close to mine. He began reading numbers off my chart, using medical terminology that I couldn't understand. Every now and then he would half turn toward the residents and they would all nod and affect wise looks. Then he would turn toward me again and read some more. I didn't know what was going on. It was as if he was presiding over some strange ritual.

"And so," he concluded, as he put the chart down, "that's why I think you probably have had a heart attack." He smiled as if he had just beaten me in a debate tournament. I expected the young doctors to start cheering.

I started to say something else, but the doctor swept out, his groupies trailing after. One glanced back with her nose in the air. I imagined I heard her say "hummmf."

The woman doctor who had assured me earlier that I wasn't

having a heart attack returned later in the morning. She entered and once again sat down on my bed. This time, she wore a long face. "I don't know how to explain this," she began, "but you may have had a heart attack. Your enzyme levels are significantly elevated, which indicates some muscle damage. We're going to do some more blood tests on you. They will tell us if the heart muscle is involved. You said that you were working out. Perhaps you damaged another muscle. We won't know for a few hours."

I felt sorry for her because she looked so sad. I felt sorry that the pompous chief doctor might be right. But mostly I felt sorry for myself. I spent a few long hours wondering what it would mean to have a heart attack before I turned fifty. I began to think of friends I knew who had had heart attacks at a young age. I thought of calling them to see how their lives had changed, but I could only remember the ones who had died. Visitors came by, trying hard not to look sad. We spent the next few hours speaking in hushed tones.

I tried to get my life in order. I didn't think that I would die, but this was surely a red flag of mortality and I vowed to live my life differently if I survived. I began making a list:

1. lose weight
2. no more ice cream
3. less work, more fun
4. worry less
5. work out more
6. lose weight

I promised to be good. I felt like someone on the *Ozzie and Harriet* show.

It was early in the afternoon when a nurse poked her head into my room and announced that I was all right. The tests had come back and they showed that the enzymes were not elevated because of my heart. "It must have been another muscle," she said as she entered. Well, I knew exactly which one. I had pulled a chest muscle on that stupid Nautilus machine trying to impress Ms. Schwarzenegger. I should add that machine to my list, I thought.

"So I can get out of here?" I asked.

"Not yet," she replied. "We want your regular doctor to discharge you and he won't be around until this evening."

"I'm not waiting," I said. "I'm leaving."

She grew thin lipped and serious. "But you can't. Your doctor has to give you permission to leave."

"But you just said that I'm OK."

"You are but it's not OK for you to leave. Right now we have an order to keep you in the hospital. Your doctor has to change that order."

"I'll sign myself out against his order."

"One minute," she said and left.

She returned with a gray-haired nurse, obviously a big cannon. "You can sign yourself out against your doctor's orders," the new nurse declared, folding her arms across her chest, "but (she paused for effect), remember if anything happens to you (another pause), if YOU DIE, we won't be responsible."

I wanted to thank her for her concern.

"Bring on the forms," I shouted, as I began to rip the little suction cups from my body. I twirled the wires around and tossed them as if I were a strip teaser. "And one for you, Chief Nurse, and here's one for the pompous doctor." I got out of the bed and began to do a bump and grind as I slowly untied the strings at the back of my gown. The nurses fled in panic.

I was so happy to be getting out. Not only hadn't I had a heart attack, but I would get home in time to tell the story to Adrienne and the kids over dinner. I was sure the story would last all the way through a three-scoop hot fudge sundae dessert.

My Mother's Love Life

At Wally's funeral, my mother acted strange. She appeared distracted and talked too loud. After the service, she demanded to see the body even though the casket was closed. She was seventy-eight, and I wondered how she'd manage now that her boyfriend was gone. Her friend Ida had introduced her to Wally eight years earlier. They might have been in their seventies at the time, but they acted like teenagers.

"Do I have a man for you," said Ida, ushering Mom into Flukey's, a neighborhood hot dog stand. "He's over there," she said, tilting her head to the left. "His name is Wally." Mom glanced over and saw a man about her age surrounded by a crowd of children and grandchildren. Wally was bald with a white fringe of hair around the edge, and he had a little pot belly. But Mom noticed his beautiful blue eyes. "Wally lost his wife a year and a half ago," Ida whispered, "and he's very lonely. He needs to go out. Wait, I'll bring him over." Before Mom could protest, Ida had leaped out of her seat and headed toward Wally. When she brought him back, she ordered him to sit. "This is my lady friend, Ruth," she began. "I want you to take her number and ask her out."

"Ida!" said my mother, nearly fainting with embarrassment. "Please." Wally left after a short conversation, which Mom thought would be the end of it.

Four days later she got a call. "I don't know if you'll remember who I am," he began hesitantly, "but you gave me your number a few days ago."

"Of course, I know who you are," replied Mom. "How many men do you think I give my number to?"

"Would you like to go to a movie with me tonight?" he asked.

"Sure," said Mom.

And so began the third great romance of her life.

The first had been with my father at age twenty. Mom dated a lot in her teens. "I was with boys ever since I was thirteen," she recalled. "There were always lots of boys around."

It's easy to understand why. Mom was a knockout. Her dark blond hair fell in soft curls around a Eastern European face with high cheekbones. She had blue-gray eyes, full red lips, and eyebrows that were so light she had to pencil them in. Her looks were classic, à la Ingrid Bergman.

Mom liked going to dances, especially when she got old enough to date guys who drove. Their favorite haunt was the Humboldt Park field house where the couples slow danced to the music of a neighborhood band. They'd also go to people's houses to sit and talk and neck. "But I wasn't wild," explained my mother. "I didn't smoke or drink. Maybe a Coke."

Her sweet sixteen party took place at her home on Crystal Street. The three-story white brick mansion was so elegant it boasted a music room with a baby grand piano. Mom wore a brown dress made for the occasion, complete with a chiffon cape on top. The girls' club she belonged to invited a boys' club from the West Side. "We turned the lights down low," she laughed, "and danced to the radio and records. Then pretty soon we were hugging and kissing in all the corners."

Mom's cousin Ruthie slept over that night. The two girls lay huddled in the same bed, laughing about some of the boys at the party, when Ruthie suddenly turned serious. "Ruth," she whispered, clutching her hand. "I think I'm pregnant."

My mother was astonished. "What happened?" she asked.

"Well, I was necking with Benny tonight," her cousin began, "and he ... he stuck his tongue in my mouth. Ruth, isn't that how it happens?" She stared at my mother, waiting for her to say something, but my mother merely shrugged. She was as ignorant about the subject as her cousin.

When they questioned their more experienced friend the next day, Pearl doubled up with laughter, then explained the facts of life to the cousins. "Can you imagine being that dumb?" mused my mother. "Sixteen and no one knew anything. Just a bunch of dumbbells. And I wasn't much better at twenty when I had my first baby. By then I knew how it got in there, but I had no idea how it was going to come out. I thought maybe it would come out through my belly button. I can tell you, I was very surprised at the truth."

Twenty was an eventful year for Mom. She got married and gave birth. But before that, she got engaged. Twice. Pete Brown, her first fiancé, was one of four brothers who worked at the family's hot dog stand. Hot dogs cost a nickel and the Brown boys—Pete, Harry, Benny, and Sam—served them slathered with flirtation. "All the girls used to walk over to Division and California for a hot dog. It was a hangout."

One day Pete sauntered over to Mom's table, put down a hot dog, and slid into the booth next to her. Pete was tall, with wavy blond hair. He was the type of guy who caused the girls to whisper together, the kind of whispers that ended with explosions of laughter. Pete was good looking and he knew it.

"What's your name?" he asked Mom, wiping his hands on the dish towel he wore slung over his shoulder.

"Ruth," answered my mother, trading glances with her girlfriend across the booth.

"Want to see a movie with me?" asked Pete, getting right down to business.

"Sure," said Mom, looking right into his eyes.

Nine months later they were engaged. That moment might have been the culmination of my mother's enchanted childhood. An only child, she'd been adored by her parents, especially her father. He bought her anything she wanted, including a pony and small surrey that they took for rides in the suburbs. Mom had grown up feeling like a princess, and Pete should have been her Prince Charming.

But even after they were engaged, Mom wasn't sure he was the one. "I don't know if I loved him," said my mother. "What did I know about love then? Now I would know if I were in love, but then I was too young. I just knew I wanted to get married. At that time if a girl was twenty and not married, she was an old maid." Little did Mom know that in the wings a second Prince Charming awaited his audition: my father.

"About two months after we got engaged," explained my mother, "Pete decided to go on a fishing trip. I told him not to leave me alone, but he wouldn't listen. And that's when I met Sammy."

Throughout her teen years, Mom had often visited the Lieberman apartment across the street from her house. My father's sister, Julia, was her girlfriend. Mom had seen my father but had never talked to him before. Pa was older with a reputation for being wild. To his family's horror, he dated only gentile girls. Mom had noticed him, of course. He dressed sharply, and his good looks carried an air of danger and excitement.

That fateful day my father lay sick in bed. My mother wore a black dress that was heavy crepe from waist to knees but sheer chiffon up top, sprinkled with glitter. The dress was so sheer she had to wear a slip under it. Like Pete, my mother was fishing, too. And that day she caught my father.

Mom found Julia playing cards with her sisters. "Go keep my

brother company," said Julia, knowing that my mother didn't play. "I'll be done soon." When Mom left, Julia leaned toward her two sisters and whispered something. The girls began to giggle.

"Come in," said Pa when my mother knocked on his door. Seeing him in bed made her shy. She didn't know what to say.

"Sit down," Pa said. "Ain't you one of Julia's girlfriends?"

"What's the matter with you?" asked Mom.

"I'm sick," he replied. "You're real pretty," he added, focusing the conversation on Mom again. "I've seen you lots of times, but I've never talked to you."

"I know that," answered Mom and they laughed.

Pa studied her for a moment and then asked, "You want to go to a wedding with me? A good friend of mine is getting married in two weeks."

"Sure," said Mom, conveniently forgetting her recent engagement.

When she came out of the bedroom a few minutes later, the Lieberman sisters peppered her with questions: What did you talk about? What did he say? Are you going out with him?

Mom pushed them away and sat down on the couch. She didn't say anything. Just smiled.

The sisters couldn't stand it. "Well?" screamed Julia.

"We're going on a date to a wedding in two weeks."

The girls shrieked and hugged my mother.

But Pa had more planned than a single date. He began by taking Mom to his hangout, the Aragon Ballroom, a dance hall on the North Side of the city.

"When you went inside, it was like you were outside," explained my mother. "They made it up to resemble a Spanish hacienda. The ceiling had twinkling lights in it like stars, and there were trees and plants scattered about. On the second floor there was a balcony where you could sit at tables, sip drinks, and watch the dancers."

Pa had been a dance instructor there, so a lot of people greeted him when he entered. They sneaked looks at Mom, sizing up Pa's newest girl. My parents slow danced to the latest offerings of Wayne King. Late in the evening as he held her close, Pa whispered in her ear, "I'm glad you know how to dance. If you didn't, I couldn't marry you."

Pa swept her off her feet. They spent their days together and went out every night. Pete Brown soon faded to a memory, a fish story about the one she threw back. The night before Pete returned, Pa asked Mom to marry him and she said yes even though she still wore Pete's ring.

Home from his fishing trip, Pete Brown burst into her apartment to find my father leaning back on the couch. Pete stopped when he saw my father. The two men eyed each other. Pa smiled arrogantly; Pete's face grew tighter by the second. "Who's this?" he asked.

"I'm getting married," said Mom. Pete looked confused, thinking she meant him. Then the truth dawned on him.

"How can you do this?" he asked. "You're engaged to me."

Mom looked from fiancé to fiancé and said, "Well, how could you leave me alone and go on a fishing trip? It just happened. I just fell in love."

"In two weeks?" Brown replied.

"It was long enough," said Pa. Brown looked from my mother to my father and then left without a word. Two weeks later my mother and father got married.

Mom wouldn't see Pete Brown again for forty-five years. After my father died, she went to visit her cousin Ruthie, who now lived in California. On Mom's first night there, her cousin came into her room and announced that they were going to a B'nai B'rith dinner dance the next night. "Pete Brown is going to be there."

"I always imagined that Pete had been pining for me all his life," said my mother. "So I got dolled up and we went to the affair."

Her cousin pointed Pete out. Age hadn't stooped him; he still stood tall. And though his hair had turned white, it remained wavy. The two women walked up and Ruthie said, "Pete, I'd like to introduce you to someone. Do you know who this is?" My mother looked up expectantly. Pete Brown studied her for a long time, a quizzical look clouding his face. "Esther Drucker?" he asked tentatively.

"Not Esther Drucker," shouted cousin Ruthie, shaking her head. "This is Ruthie Klein!"

"Oh my God," said Pete. "Ruthie Klein. Oh my God." When he introduced Mom to his wife, he referred to Mom as "the love of my life."

"Sure," recalled Mom disgustedly, "the love of his life. He didn't even recognize me. Esther Drucker! Esther Drucker didn't even look like me; she was a short, dark girl. There's no comparison."

Mom might have made a snap decision to marry my father, and she might have questioned her gamble on a gambler, but my parents remained married for thirty-five years. Of course, these years changed Mom. You can see it when you thumb through old photographs.

The early photographs show a beautiful woman with wavy hair, a curvaceous figure, and a saucy look on her face. In one photograph, she poses like a '40s movie star with one hand on her hip and a sexy smirk on her face that dares you to take her picture.

In later photographs she wears a more matronly look—her cheeks have filled out and her smile has softened. In most shots, she's posing at the beach or at the park surrounded by her three young sons.

As her sons get taller, she looks the same except that her hair turns platinum blond. In her fifties, she gets plump and dons glasses. Her hairline recedes. By her sixties, she's wearing a blond wig and has begun to look like the grandmother she is.

But while Mom's appearance changed, her desirability never waned. Nine months after my father died, the second great love of her life, Maury, moved in. Mom met Maury a month after Pa's funeral. Maury had played cards with Pa at the neighborhood card joint in the back of a cigar store. One day he helped Mom home with her groceries. "So we began going places together," said Mom. "Naturally, when his lease ran out, I invited him to stay with me." He stayed eleven years until he died.

"Maury was a good man. He took me places; we had lots of fun. And we never fought. Whenever I would get mad, he would walk out until I cooled off. I would yell after him, 'Coward, come and fight with me,' but he would just walk out without a word. I'd see him strolling up and down in front of the house waiting for me to calm down."

"When Pa died, he left nothing but debts. He'd gambled away everything. But when Maury died, he left me everything he had in his two checking accounts. And then one day when I went to make the bed, I flipped the sheets in the air and all these dollar bills started flying around the room. He had kept a hundred dollars tucked between the mattress and the bedsprings and didn't even tell me. It was like his final good-bye."

Three years later, Mom met Wally. She had been manless for the whole time, unless you count Mr. Colen. Mom had known Mr. and Mrs. Colen for over forty years. After Mrs. Colen died, Mom and Mr. Colen began to keep company. But Mr. Colen's idea of a day out was taking her to the cemetery so they could visit their dead spouses. It made for a peculiar double date.

Mr. Colen was surprised when my mother sent him a birthday card. He couldn't figure out how she knew his birthday. "Of course,

I know," she told him. "I've seen it on your tombstone a dozen times.

"I didn't really like him as a boyfriend," Mom said. "He was a little man and I always felt like a giant next to him. Anyway, I can't like a man who doesn't enjoy eating. He used to make chicken soup for himself by putting two *pulkeys* (drumsticks), a carrot, an onion, and a piece of celery in some water. What kind of a soup is that? And then he told me that he would get two meals out of it because he only eats one drumstick at a time."

My mother was ecstatic when she met Wally. He had all the qualities she was looking for in a man now that she was seventy. "He's got all his teeth, he likes to eat, and he can drive at night. He's perfect," she told me.

"At first we started going out once a week," she explained. "But soon it was twice. Then it got to be three times a week, and then it got to be every day of the week."

Wally loved to go places and that suited my mom. If she mentioned that she read about a mall opening, they were dressed and out the door. They flew to California and Florida to visit relatives. Their whirlwind courtship never slowed down. They were like teenagers.

And like teenagers, they were thinking about sex. "It's always been important to me," said my Mom. "I had lots of experience. Pete Brown, your father, Maury, and Wally. What do you think, when people are in their seventies, there's no sex? There's sex in your seventies," she added with a laugh. "When there's a spark, it's hard to be platonic.

"When you get older, the men have a hard time, but they try. Wally and I had a good sex life. He used to tell me that I taught him more than he ever knew in his whole life. I can't imagine how he was doing it before. We had some thrills."

After five years they decided to get married, but then Wally developed trouble walking. The doctors discovered a malignant tumor on his spine. The marriage plans were put on hold and Mom moved in to help nurse him. Wally's condition declined until finally he was confined to a wheelchair. Then a stroke hospitalized him.

I visited him with Mom right after the stroke. Wally couldn't talk, but from the tears in his eyes I knew how happy he was to see her.

"You had a stroke, Wally," said Mom, leaning toward him. He strained to say something but he couldn't get it out.

"What?" asked Mom. "What are you trying to say? Can you write it down?" She found a piece of paper and a pen in her purse and pushed it toward him, but he was unable to handle the pen.

She rubbed his swollen arm. "Feel this," she said to me. "It doesn't feel like skin. Are you cold, Wally? You feel cold?"

The whole time Wally looked at her with pleading eyes, desperate to say something. He weakly motioned her toward him. She leaned close, and turned her ear to his mouth, thinking he would whisper something. When she did, Wally kissed her on the cheek.

"He kissed me," said my mother, holding her cheek. "He kissed me." A few weeks later he died.

AFTER SPENDING HER LIFE WITH MEN, what would my seventy-eight-year-old mother do now that she was alone?

Two days after the funeral, our family headed over to Wally's house, where his family sat *shiva.* That's the Jewish custom of setting aside a week for people to gather in order to remember the deceased and comfort the bereaved.

The place overflowed with relatives and friends. We found Mom in a corner by the dining room table. "Have something to eat," she said when we walked up. "We've got so much food here. Everyone who comes over brings something, and they ordered two big trays of food from a delicatessen. Eat. Go ahead."

"How are you doing?" Adrienne asked.

Mom shrugged as if to say, "How can I be doing?" As she talked about how hard the funeral had been, I began to feel more at ease. She seemed in better control of herself than she had been on the day of the funeral. We passed the time with small talk, the crowd around us alternately falling quiet or breaking into laughter. People kept coming over to shake Mom's hand and tell her how sorry they were.

Finally, when the room cleared out a little, Mom, with an odd smile on her face, beckoned us toward her. We leaned forward, looking as if we were huddling up. "Guess what?" she whispered. "One of Wally's friends called me up. He said that he always wanted to get to know me, but he couldn't because I was taken. But now that I'm available ...." She shrugged, not needing to finish the thought.

Adrienne put her hand on Mom's hand and said, "Ruth, you're irresistible."

Mom smiled again. "That's just the word he used."

The new relationship never materialized. They went on a few breakfast dates, but her new beau, an eighty-year-old bachelor, decided he was too busy with his eighty-five-year-old sister's family to go out. When he called and told Mom, she hung up on him. "Who needs him?" she said. "He likes to play solitaire. Do you believe that? He sits in his house and plays solitaire. I mean, what the hell is that? These are the last years of our lives. Go out and live it up. Do something. Damn it, get yourself a woman and go out and have a good time.

"I need a younger man," she mused. "Look at the movie stars. They're all marrying younger men. I don't want some crotchety old guy at this stage of the game. I want someone who can still get around, who can still see, who can still eat. Someone who knows how to live."

She laughed as if surprised at her own audacity. She might be a seventy-eight-year-old grandmother in a blond wig, but inside danced a saucy teenager surrounded by boyfriends, a young woman who'd been engaged to two men at the same time, a showy platinum blond. She was still a woman who loved men and loved being loved by them. She'd buried three great loves, and hearing her laugh, I couldn't help but feel that the fourth might be waiting in the wings.

"Mom, I think you're going to be all right," I said, patting her hand.

"Sure," she replied, patting me back.

Other Books from August House Publishers

Through a Ruby Window

A Martha's Vineyard Childhood

Susan Klein

Hardback $19.95 / ISBN 0-87483-416-3

The Farm on Nippersink Creek

Stories from a Midwestern Childhood

Jim May

Paperback $18.95 / ISBN 0-87483-339-6

Once upon a Galaxy

The ancient stories that inspired Star Wars, Superman, and other popular fantasies

Josepha Sherman

Hardback $19.95 / ISBN 0-87483-386-8

Paperback $11.95 / ISBN 0-87483-387-6

The Storyteller's Start-Up Book

Finding, Learning, Performing, and Using Folktales

Margaret Read MacDonald

Hardback $23.95 / ISBN 0-87483-304-3

Paperback $13.95 / ISBN 0-87483-305-1

Queen of the Cold-Blooded Tales

Roberta Simpson Brown

Paperback $9.95 / ISBN 0-87483-408-2

Race with Buffalo

and Other Native American Stories for Young Readers

Collected by Richard and Judy Dockrey Young

Hardback $19.95 / ISBN 0-87483-343-4

Paperback $9.95 / ISBN 0-87483-342-6